Praise for

The Landlord of Hummingbird House

"An honest and heartfelt novel of personal connection, layer by layer.

Jane Harvey's The Landlord of Hummingbird House is a story of the quiet yet biting sense of imposter syndrome. This contemporary novel is cosy and warm while addressing real discomforts, regrets, and traumas.

Harvey's writing is descriptive as opposed to prescriptive, capturing people in all their simplicity and depth without being moralizing. It unravels outward appearances, suggesting that immediate perceptions may prevent, or at least delay, meaningful connection."

Independent Book Review

The Landlord of Hummingbird House

Jane Harvey

FIRST EDITION

Book design by Dreena Collins
Vectors, Canva

ISBN 978-1-9196023-3-2

For anyone who has had to start again.

Chapter One:
April

He was sitting on the wall outside the house. Not at all like she had expected. His grey t-shirt was distressed and raw-edged, the short sleeves taut around his biceps. The sharp point of a black tattoo poked out from beneath the fabric on his left arm.

He was poised, still, hands clasped together as he stared straight ahead.

April parked as close as she could, her little Fiat squeezing neatly into the last remaining space on that side of the street. She got out, grabbing her phone and keys but leaving behind the Tetris stack of boxes and bags that filled the car.

As she walked towards him, he didn't move even though he must have heard her approaching. It was peculiar, really. She couldn't put her finger on what else it was that seemed so odd. But there was something majestic about him. So centred and still.

He wasn't playing with a phone, she realised, with a jolt.

"Hi!" she called when she was just a couple of metres away.

He turned his head towards her but kept the rest of his body still. He had stubble, but not a full beard, thankfully. Why these men insisted on hiding their jaws with beards was a mystery to her.

Not that it mattered whether he had a beard or not, of course. Even if there was something striking about him, she was only meeting him for the keys.

He didn't smile; seemed to stare right through her and out the other side, blue eyes cold and clear.

"April, I assume," he said.

"The one and only!" she answered, for some unknown reason. "Ha!" she laughed, trying to cover up her awkwardness, but only adding to it.

He looked at her for a beat too long, and she was suddenly self-conscious; wished she had done something more glamorous with her hair. His was dark, almost black, wavy and a little wild. One strand flopped down across his forehead and almost reached his eyelashes.

"Follow me," was all he said in response.

It seemed bizarre to be moving into a flat she hadn't even viewed, but such was the property market these days. She'd learned the hard way that there was no scope for 'sleeping on it' or leaving things a day or two. All the best flats went within hours. She had taken this one on the basis of the pictures alone. She hoped he wasn't too hot with Photoshop.

The house looked slightly tired, with faded red brick and a few brave weeds fighting their way through broken slabs, but it was undeniably pretty, and somehow impressive. It was three storeys high, and the upper half of some basement windows suggested another flat below. The doorway and window trims were painted white, and well maintained, she noticed. The majority of the other homes in the terrace had replaced their small front yards with parking spaces. In spite of the potential inconvenience, April was pleased by the creak of the black metal gate as her guide pushed it open. And she liked the pointed bars standing guard on top of the gate, and the fence that bordered the house. There was a tidy row of well-maintained potted plants up against the wall in the tiny yard, next to an old bench. She paused outside the front door and looked up to take in the building.

"Georgian," he muttered.

"What?" she asked, unsure if she had heard him properly.

"It's *Georgian*. The house." He was visibly irritated.

"Right-o," she said. She knew this already but didn't want to play architectural bingo with him. The restrained but stately stucco around the door, the neat uniform design of the tall houses on the brick terrace made it obvious. But she wasn't going to tell him so, as he looked annoyed enough already. Besides, he was halfway into the hallway while she had continued to stand there, staring skywards. She'd have to examine the house front later, it seemed.

She followed him in. The hall was simple: tidy and clean, carpeted in a neutral beige. Absently, she wondered if there were still tiles underneath.

"Post," he gestured to a shelf of cubby holes labelled from 'Basement' to 'Four'. Then he was off again.

"You're on the next floor. Number three."

"Yes," she said, nervous of saying something foolish again. Best keep it brief.

The key was already in the keyhole when they reached the flat. He had pounded ahead of her, hopping up the stairs adeptly. He stood waiting for her, and she found herself a little too close to him once she caught up, trapped as they were in the narrow corridor. She could feel the warmth of him. Hear him breathing. She looked up, and he was staring at her – those sharp blue eyes under a furrowed brow. What was happening? He leaned forward, even closer, and lifted his right arm. She could see the tendons flexing in his forearm, fluctuating, and rippling like the strings of a grand piano. She noted how large his hands were. She wondered if he was about to touch her face.

He tapped gently on the flat's door with his index finger.

"After you," he said.

He was expecting her to let them in. Into her flat. She blushed. There was that foolishness again.

"Right-o!" she said. Where had this new phrase appeared from?

The door was light and opened straight into the apartment, which was exactly as it had appeared in the pictures. Thank God.

So, this was it. Her new home. Hummingbird House.

*

When she was seventeen, April spent many evenings walking home because she'd used her taxi fare on a last round of drinks. Then she'd eat half a loaf of toast in the kitchen with a friend who had tagged along. A different friend each week.

Hung over, sleep deprived, the next day she would take huge sheets of flipchart paper and draw bright, abstract images in wax pastels. Crimson waves and blue one-eyed dragons stared back at her, supposedly embodying the feelings, the pure joy of the night. Her inner life, on paper, she'd say.

On reflection, she was probably insufferable.

Eighteen, and she managed to scrape average A-Level grades; a mixture of high potential and below par effort plonking her slap in the middle of mediocrity. Her parents sighed, though in some respects were relieved. It was a wake-up call of sorts, and she'd learned her lesson, mostly; though at university it wasn't unheard of for her to be found walking the back streets, eating chips at 2 am, or staying up until three to make an essay deadline.

She got a 2:1. Almost – though not quite – a First.

History of Art.

The year after her degree, she moved to Edinburgh with her boyfriend, Stefan. He was studying for a Masters degree while she worked two jobs (but never seemed to have any money). It was a disaster. You can imagine.

She moved back home eight months later; didn't eat properly for another two. By the time the summer came around again, she had lost so much weight that the rebound sex with Billy-the-Barman left him bruised – her body a concertina of clavicles and elbows. It took her another six months to lift her confidence enough to realise she was far too thin, and Billy was far too dim.

April learned her lesson that time, too, and she was more cautious with men going forward. She would not be moving over three hundred miles for anyone. And she had no intention of working two crappy jobs simultaneously ever again.

She went back to college, became a primary school teacher, and then shared a house with her big sister,

Kelly.

That was the peak, really. Her pinnacle. She and Kelly were a deadly duo at that time: cheeky, lively, and utterly trusting of one another. That faith in each other was still there now, and she would trust Kelly with her life. But time had moved on and things were different now in immeasurable ways.

Back then, she had been happy. Simply happy. Unencumbered. She lived for each individual day, joyfully. It was a sort of extended youth with no mortgage or responsibilities, less body hair, and sitcom levels of independence and fun. She was still on the slim side, too: youth, hard work and the remnants of earlier weight loss in her favour. Of course, that's pretty shallow, of course it is, but at least she didn't feel self-conscious, unhealthy, ashamed.

And nothing scared her in those days.

Nothing.

*

An hour later, she was making her fourth trip up the stairs, wondering again why she hadn't asked her sister to help with the move. Or anyone, in fact. Her humiliation at being single once more, starting over at the age of thirty-two, had meant she'd been acting as if this was nothing. At least, publicly she had. Yet she knew she fooled no one. And there were many reasons why it was ridiculous to pretend otherwise. Not least that it would have meant fewer trips up these damn stairs.

She was balancing a potted Dracaena on top of a box of vinyl when she heard someone on the landing. Not him again, she hoped. She didn't think she could

6

face another round of "Right-os!" and steely stares.

"Do you need a hand?"

She tried to turn her head towards the voice, but she was mid-key-turn, and her chin was wedged in a Dragon Tree, so it wasn't going to happen.

The key jammed; she found she didn't have the grip or force to get it to turn all the way around. As she tried to wiggle it, globules of warm sweat oozing from her forehead, she could hear someone approaching. Someone light of foot. Then a man's hand came into view. It gently but forcibly took the key from her and turned it confidently in the lock. He pushed the door open, and she stumbled forwards into the flat.

Once the box and plant were safely on the floor, she was finally able to look at her helper, taking in his checked shirt and navy trousers, sensible brogues. His hair was clipped short, almost buzzed off, slightly flecked with grey. He could have been anything from twenty-five to forty. He had a face that could easily be forgotten. But there was a hint of a smile there.

"Thank you," she managed. "I am not usually incapable of opening doors, honest."

He shrugged. "They do take some getting used to, these locks. I still have trouble sometimes."

He was trying to be nice, she guessed, but a full day's worth of humiliation was hanging over her and she couldn't help but feel patronised.

"I'm sure I'll get the hang of it," she said.

He nodded. He was still in the doorway and she wondered if she should invite him in. But she really didn't want to.

"I'm April," she ventured. "New neighbour, in case you hadn't realised."

"Paul," he said. "Number two."

For some ridiculous reason this made her giggle. That's what happens when your daily grind revolves around seven-year-olds. He smiled more broadly. She wasn't sure if it was a sincere grin, or a polite one.

He said, "Do you have any more to bring up?"

"Thankfully, there's not much left. I think I'm OK to leave it in the car for now. Can't see burglars being desperate for an unused Crock-Pot and a second-hand copy of *The Handmaid's Tale*. But thanks."

He glanced around briefly, and she wondered if he noted how little she had with her.

"Yes, er... I think you'll be safe," he said. But he remained standing there, and she found herself grappling for things to say to fill the gap; she wished he'd just back off and leave her to it. She'd had too much awkward small talk for one day.

"I've met the landlord," she said. He raised his eyebrows. She chuckled. "He's quite something, isn't he?" and she flicked her head upwards, indicating the floor above.

"Oh, Dai? He won't give you any bother."

"Die?" she laughed. "That's a hell of a name. Rather suits him." It sounded more bitter than she intended.

"Welsh," he said, and turned to go.

"Right-o!" she said.

Chapter Two:
Paul

As he entered his flat, he noted there was a faint smell of garlic still in the air. It bothered him; lowered his mood. It had been three days since he'd roasted the bulb, and he'd tried all manner of things to get rid of the remnants of its scent, now somewhat sour and salty. The rubbish had been removed immediately; the kitchen cleaned straight away, of course. He had opened all the windows; burned a dozen candles (of which he usually thoroughly disapproved); squirted artificial air fresheners that claimed to take the smell away and not just mask it.

It served him right. He knew better than to cook smelly food.

He walked to the back of the flat and entered the kitchen, then pressed the button on his bean-to-cup machine. Perhaps the scent of coffee beans would help to disguise the garlic. While the machine went through its creaks and groans, he cautiously pulled out the drip tray and tipped it into the sink. A small waterfall of brown residue fell onto the ceramic, and he flinched as he saw the dark specks of coffee grind splatter, peppering the white. He rinsed the sink with the hose from the tap. He'd had to persuade them to allow him to install that; did it at his own expense in the end, even though this was a rental. It was worth it.

He thought back to his youth; wondered what young Paul would have made of this. When he was seventeen, eighteen, he was perhaps an unusual character as even then he had a tidy bedroom and a sensible haircut. No gel or fashion statements for him. But even so, he had never imagined that he would turn out to be the sort of thirty-five-year-old to have an impressive selection of drainer cleaner and three different types of mop.

As he moved efficiently between cupboards, collecting his favourite mug, his favourite spoon, his favourite coaster, the milk jug, a clean white tea towel, he reflected on the new tenant. April, she said her name was. She was a funny thing, jumping between warm and open, and overtly hostile. He wondered if he'd made a fool of himself. He had stood there a moment too long, he knew it. But, even though he wasn't sure he actually warmed to her, she was interesting, so he hadn't wanted to leave. He didn't get to experience much of any interest at the moment. Life was mundane. He sighed. That was his own fault, of course. At first, it had been about self-preservation and was how he had liked it. Now, it was more like a habit. Fear too, possibly.

Perhaps he would knock on her door and invite her for coffee. Perhaps – though it seemed remarkably unlikely. He let the daydream set in: pictured himself laughing with her as they unpacked her boxes and chatted about her life, her world, her friends. She was bound to have much to share. And he would get to know her to see if she was as interesting as she first appeared.

Most people weren't, in his experience. Dramatic maybe; difficult, certainly. But even those things can become routine and predictable in their way.

He thought back to the last tenant of number three. The flat had been empty for two or three months this year but prior to that there had been a young man there: Joe. His family – a catalogue of miniature Joes and giant Joes, hard to tell apart – had helped him move in one weekend and, although they had teased and bantered their way up and down the stairs together, they didn't respond to Paul's attempt to strike up conversation. Paul had learned the hard way that it would have been worth pushing this point and making sure they could at least say hello, as Joe and he had spent the next few months doing little more than nod at each other when they passed on the stairs. Those very narrow stairs.

Towards the end of Joe's nine-month tenancy, Paul had even taken to trying to avoid using the staircase at the same time as him, listening out, sometimes even checking through a crack in the door, and then hiding behind his flat door until the coast was clear.

It was important to push through social awkwardness, sometimes, for the long-term good. He would do that with April. He would. He would make sure they could at least say hello, if nothing else. And maybe they would even chat on occasion.

One thing was clear, anyway: she didn't think much of Dai.

Chapter Three:
April

April spent that evening sat on a coverless duvet stuffed into a bin bag. She had her one special chair, of course, but it was piled high with books and a random box of kitchen utensils. She couldn't be bothered to move it all; was happy to drink her lager on the floor. It was her floor, and she appreciated it.

She had done very little after her neighbour left. She'd intended to continue with lifting and sorting but after she had stopped to chat, she realised how thirsty she was and had taken what was intended to be a break, but soon developed into a downing of tools. First, she had tea and water. The teabag was still in the sink, swollen and burst. Now she was on her second beer, alongside a dinner of peanuts and an overripe banana. But why not? It had been a long day.

She took in the flat. Dimming now as evening set in, the light in this room had been bright and airy for most of the day. The ceilings were high and dramatic. It had been good timing for her (using the term 'good' in its loosest possible sense, of course) to be moving in during the school summer holidays. The large, deep windows faced south and, as she was on the first floor, she was considering having no blinds or sheers to cover them. It would be a shame to do so, as they made the room. Perhaps in the bedroom, which had less of the light anyway, but not here. Not in this wonderful space.

April thought perhaps she had actually landed on her feet.

The living room, where she was now, had a real hardwood floor, and a fireplace. Not functioning and in fact not very picturesque as, at some stage, the chimney breast had been boxed around and there was no mantle or hearth. But there was still a hole in the wall, an alcove where the fire should be, and a cast-iron decorative grate. There was a sturdy picture hook above it, mourning the loss of artwork that had clearly hung there once, and calling to her to find some more. She was already dreaming of how lovely it would be when her scented candles were placed in the cavity. She wondered how old the floorboards were. They didn't seem to be a DIY addition; perhaps they were the real thing.

Of course, the rest of the flat didn't match up to this standard. The dated kitchen units had clearly been painted over at some point, and the now blue cupboards showed glimpses of beige beneath. One of them even had the remnants of children's stickers on it, half-peeled and fluffy, stubbornly dotted and scarring the surface. The kitchen tiles had a peculiar brown and beige pattern to them.

The bathroom was even worse, with a mustard yellow suite and a cracked sink. No windows, but a noisy fan that clattered and vibrated for at least ten minutes after use.

It was lucky for her that this was the case because the flat would have been well out of her price range if it had wooden floors and original features throughout.

It was the first time she had lived alone for —

actually, she had never lived alone, she realised. She had been reminiscing about her time at university whenever the idea of a one-bed flat came up, but of course she hadn't lived alone at uni. Not really. She had never lived in a one-bedroom flat, but in a hall of residence where doors were propped open, and meals eaten together. And she'd had no furniture, utility bills, or responsibilities of her own. It was far removed from this.

The only thing reminiscent of that time was her ongoing inability to get her act together and learn how to make a proper dinner.

Tom had cooked their meals for the last six years — when they weren't eating out or having a take-away, that is. On the rare nights when she was in charge of the kitchen, she usually cooked up a ready-made pizza. He used to laugh at this. At first. Back when he used to laugh.

Perhaps that was the challenge she should set herself: to learn how to cook.

And to learn how to be alone.

*

Over the next ten days, April continued to set up, making the flat a home. She moved the box and bits from her one chair, eventually, and cleaned the kitchen cupboards, and unpacked. Her blue rug fitted nicely in the kitchen and cheered up the small space. She made a mental note to go shopping for more bits and pieces for the other rooms.

In the living room, there were three shelves, which she filled with books. She would eventually place some photographs there too, she imagined, but at the moment something stopped her – the permanency, or how it highlighted the loneliness of her situation, perhaps – she wasn't sure. No matter. She didn't have to do everything at once, she reminded herself. One step at a time.

She also made sure to find out who else lived in this house-cum-block-of-flats with her. She had never been good with names, so she made herself a chart and put names and key words next to flat numbers on a not-to-scale map, and gave it pride of place on her fridge, bolted on by a mermaid fridge magnet that was a gift from her niece. When Kelly came around to inspect the premises, she referred to it as April's 'hit list', laughing that she had even made a note of the cat on the ground floor.

Dai seemed to be the only person who lived on the top floor, though she had not dared to venture up there, having no legitimate excuse were she to be spotted. But it was almost always quiet above her. She had never heard voices through the floor, only the faint thud of music on occasion and what sounded like someone exercising. It seemed likely that his flat was larger, then, although he appeared to live alone. Two-bed, no doubt, as it took up the whole floor. Which of course made sense, as it was his house.

She'd only seen him in person once since that first day. She was coming out of her flat mid-morning, and he had been taking the stairs two at a time, wearing a black vest top and some scruffy tracksuit bottoms that were too big, sitting low on his firm waist. The little rope of muscle at the top of his hips poked over the top of the trousers. He was beaded with sweat on his shoulders, she saw as he jogged past her, saying nothing while she fiddled with that damn key. She could smell him in the hallway, a mix of warm fresh sweat and men's deodorant. And something woody, she thought. Maybe sandalwood.

The ground floor also had only one flat. That was occupied by Jonty and Ben, a couple in their forties or fifties who had greeted April enthusiastically, vowing to have her around to drink Merlot and meet their decrepit cat, Oxo. Jonty referred to them as 'the grandads' – a nod to the fact they were older than the other residents, but also that they were the longest-serving tenants.

"We've been here decades, love. We know all the secrets of this house." He leaned in and winked conspiratorially. She had been inside once already – they often had their front window, or even their flat door open as she passed. Their place was bursting with old wooden furniture and bookcases laden with hardback books. And there was a piano that, so far, she hadn't heard anyone play. Oxo seemed to have claimed the seat as his own.

"Well, you don't know any of mine yet, I hope," she smiled.

"Maybe not, but I am a master detective, and it won't take me long to work them out," Jonty replied.

"It's true, April. He is. He's a nosy bugger."

April laughed, but felt uneasy. She wasn't ready to share her past just yet.

The truth was they weren't the eldest tenants, April discovered. That accolade belonged to Betty Williams, who resided in the basement flat. Betty looked to be somewhere in her late seventies, maybe older. She had also made April feel at home, greeting her joyously, clapping her hands together and saying she hoped April had moved in alright, and that Dai had given her a warm welcome. She said this with a twinkle that was hard to fathom. Gentle sarcasm? Teasing? Insinuation? April wasn't sure, but she warmed to Betty anyway, passing her often as she sat on the old bench at the front of the house drinking a cup of tea from a china mug and fishing treats from her pockets to share with Oxo.

April was glad some of the neighbours seemed normal, at least. And pleased that it wasn't a house of twenty-something party freaks. All in all, she was happy with her home. As happy as she could be, under the circumstances.

Chapter Four:
Dai

Betty Williams was a good sort, and he forced himself to accept her suggestion of tea and cake when she offered. Payback for him collecting her new flat-pack wardrobe from the industrial estate, she said. But it had been no bother. He needed excuses to get out and about. It was good for him. He was well aware this was the case, but struggled to do it anyway, and this was probably the very reason she had asked him to run the errand for her.

"Would offer to put it together for you," he said. "But I am useless. Really awful."

Betty laughed. "I wasn't going to ask. I remember what happened when you agreed to put that extra bolt on my door."

Dai winced, pictured the multiple holes in the door frame where he had repeatedly misaligned everything. They had all laughed at that, but it still stung. "Me, too."

He hadn't realised she was planning on bringing the tea outside. Of course she would be, she always did. He watched as she moved towards the stairs and took pains to navigate them carefully with the tray. Wordlessly, he took the tray from her, wondering how she managed it on a daily basis. She didn't object. He followed her up the stairs and out of the front door into the little paved area.

Dai was standing, teacup in one hand, cake balanced on the edge of a planter, when the guys from number one opened their bedroom window and leaned out.

"Having a party without us? How dare you!" Jonty cried.

Betty chuckled. "You're welcome to join us. There's more fruit cake."

"And that's just the company!" quipped Jonty.

Dai looked to the ground.

Jonty and Ben pulled their curtains fully open and, staying inside, leaned against their window, drinking fizzy drinks and teasing Betty. They talked about a local theatre production, segued into a Radio 4 drama, and then onto a story about the time they visited Aberystwyth and Jonty twisted his ankle climbing the hill in less than sensible shoes while sporting a hangover.

Dai wondered how it was some people found it this easy, this simple, to chat and laugh and make themselves at home. It was entertaining, but most of it was fluffy nonsense. Written down, you would wonder why on earth they bothered to chat about it at all. It didn't matter. They all seemed so happy, joining in, chuckling and teasing one another. The point was to interact and to laugh, not to share knowledge or say something clever, he supposed. He wondered if that skill was something you learned or was simply something you had. Innate. He also wondered if he had ever had it. He couldn't remember ever being that way.

"Here comes trouble!" called Ben, as Dai registered footsteps approaching.

He looked up to see April walking a little white dog, and accompanied by another young woman with shiny dark hair, like April's but cut shorter and smarter than hers. This friend wore proper shoes with those funny wedge heels, and a floaty scarf thing around her shoulders. April was in flip flops and short denim skirt.

She smiled at Ben. "Speak for yourself," she said, before turning to Dai. "Don't worry, it's not my dog."

He stared at her a moment and then shrugged, unsure how to respond. Did she think he was scared?

"It's a Lhasa," he said.

"That's right!" said April's friend, surprised. "Do you have a dog?"

Dai shook his head with one swift movement and looked away, having nothing more to add to this conversation. He did not have a dog. He had never had a dog. He turned back to his cake.

"Aren't you going to introduce us to your sister?" Jonty asked.

April's mouth dropped open. "Jeez, you were right about the sleuthing skills. There's no getting anything past you."

"You don't have to be Sherlock to make that connection," he replied. "You're practically twins."

Dai looked at them again briefly, and realised Jonty was right: they were clearly sisters, but not twins. There was something unusual about April, something insubstantial, intangible but nice, that the other girl didn't have. Not to the same degree. Though she was striking and neat, in a different way.

April introduced her sister to everyone, and the volume rose as familiarity increased, and, of course, teasing followed, until he wondered how much longer he had to stay, whether it would be rude to go now.

The dog was on a loose lead and started to explore the slabs and plant pots, sniffing at legs and weeds. The front patio was pretty and well-tended, with an array of colours and scents, but the slabs needed repointing, and there were many nooks and crannies amongst the pots: no doubt appealing to a little dog. At one point, he cocked a leg and sprayed a tinkle of yellow onto a planter. Everyone laughed.

And then Paul appeared, carrying a brown paper bag and a newspaper. So that was everyone. All of them. He stood near April and even he seemed comfortable there. Even Paul.

So Dai simply said: "Well. Bye, then," to no one in particular and rushed back in through the front door.

He could hear them all chatting — Paul, April, her sister, and Betty — for at least another hour through the crack in his living room window, while he lay on his couch in silence and tried to remember to breathe.

Chapter Five:
April

Saturday morning, and Kelly arrived at 10 am, knocking straight on the flat door. April was still sleepy, wearing lounge pants and a baggy t-shirt which were hardly more formal than the pyjamas she'd taken off twenty minutes earlier. It was a pretence at being dressed and ready, at least, even if she wasn't actually showered.

"I come bearing curtains," Kelly said, as soon as April opened the door, "And croissants."

"Both useful things," April said. She stepped to the side and let her in, trying to smooth her hair with one hand, shamed by Kelly's shiny bob.

"Late night?" Kelly asked, leaning in to look at her.

"Not especially. But, for once, I actually slept." She closed the door. "And of course, now I feel groggy as hell. That's the way it is, isn't it? Anyway, I didn't expect you just yet."

"Ugh. Sorry... feels like lunchtime to me. Olive's been up since five-thirty. Again."

April winced in sympathy. Olive had never been a good sleeper but, since turning four, for some reason she seemed to be getting worse. The thought of being woken by an enthusiastic and chatty child at that time made April feel ill.

"Coffee?" she offered.

"I'll make it." Kelly walked past her towards the kitchen. "You look even worse than I feel."

*

Armed with a large mug of coffee and two croissants, April felt more able to converse. She was perched on the duvet seat, leaving the one chair for Kelly. Her plate was on the floor.

"Who let you in, anyway?" she asked, hoping no one was in the habit of leaving the front door open. It was a safe neighbourhood, she was sure, but a little more down-at-heel than where she had been living, lately, and she didn't quite feel secure yet.

"Your neighbour. Not the International-Man-of-Mystery, the other bloke with the short hair. I didn't recognise him at first, but he reminded me we'd met out front. Oops... I blamed it on 'mummy brain', though that excuse is wearing thin since she's been walking and talking."

April nodded. "And potty trained, and counting, and —"

"OK., don't rub it in. Until I am getting more than five hours sleep a night, that's my excuse, and I'm sticking to it."

"Fair enough. I get brain fog even without that excuse, to be honest. I hope for your sake she's not in this phase much longer, sis."

Kelly closed her eyes and scrunched up her face. April saw for a moment just how tired she was, and vowed to help out more.

"So, how long do I have you for? I've a list of jobs as long as my arm," she said, changing the subject.

Kelly looked around. "You look pretty settled in, to

me."

"That illusion is created by the lack of things to unpack. Of course there are no bags and boxes, as I have nothing. I own nothing. You know that. But I'd still like to get this flat sorted. You know what it's like – I strongly suspect that if I don't do it all now, I'll still have no curtains in the bedroom this time next year."

"Ugh, yes. I do know that feeling. We have some boxes of books in the garage from when we bought the house, three years ago."

April smiled. "Luckily for you, for once I am motivated to get this sorted this summer rather than sometime in the next decade, so there are quite a few odd jobs to do about the place."

"Yes, lucky me. Well, I'm happy to help. But I hope they are easy. I'm not as handy as you are."

"Oh yes," April nodded. "I am a diligent foreman. I shall only delegate what is within your skill set."

"My limited skill set?" Kelly asked. "Anyway, I'm quite excited to be doing adult things on a weekend for once. I've got two or three hours. But Russ wants to see his mum this afternoon, so I'd best not be too late."

"I'd better get you to work, then," April smiled, ruefully.

She had an impressive stash of tools that she kept in the airing cupboard for want of a better place. They were among the few things she'd been keen to take with her when she left Tom. He'd never once used them, but she was strangely attached to them. Next to her toolbox was a new shelf, still in its cellophane, and a cupboard box containing sandpaper, white spirits, and paint.

Kelly peered in. "I'll do the curtains, shall I?

24

Bedroom?"

"Right-uh... I mean, yes, great." April picked up the box and carried it to the kitchen where she turned on the radio.

They worked in different rooms, and the murmur of the radio plus the distance, meant they laboured in silence for much of the time. Kelly fed through dozens of curtain hooks, first in the bedroom and then at the back of the living room, while April sanded the kitchen units with gusto. A cloud of blue paint filled the air, and she was glad she'd remembered to put dust cloths down. It was absorbing, rhythmical, scrubbing at the old paint. And there was something rewarding in seeing the surfaces turn matt and smooth under the pressure of her hands.

When she and Tom had bought their flat, she had been the one to do this kind of work. It was a ground floor flat with a small patio to the rear and, although it was a modern building and structurally sound, the decor was dated. Tom had wanted them to get in a redecorating company and blitz the place before they even moved in, but a difficult evening of bookkeeping made it clear this wasn't an option. Once they'd paid the deposit and fees, and bought a new sofa and bed, there was little left. He looked horrified, completely amazed, by the idea of doing it up themselves; as if it had never occurred to him that people did such things. She'd laughed, reached over his shoulder, shut the laptop screen, and squeezed him tight.

"I'm pretty nifty with a paintbrush," she had said.

And, as it turned out, that was true. Some of it came naturally to her, the rest was easy enough to learn via the internet. She took straight to 'cutting in' the edges and the ceiling without tape or a second thought. Tom was amazed, asking her how she knew what to do. She just did. She looked at things and could see how they worked, more often than not. And if she didn't, she wanted to find out.

Tom had no interest, and found it amusing that she wanted to spend her half-term holidays re-grouting tiles and her weekends steam-cleaning things. She even worked on it during term time, when the kids at school ran her off her feet with a forty- to fifty-hour week. But, in all honesty, she loved to see the results of her work. It was good, at first, that Tom didn't want to help: it had been a long time since she'd been able to do something, make something, and say it was all hers. No one else had done this. Only her. She felt proud.

Somehow, though, she'd always vaguely imagined she'd make headway and then he'd follow her lead. That she'd be showing him what to do once she'd learned it herself. But that didn't happen.

At first, he bought her cups of tea, rubbed her shoulders at the end of a long day. He would even come with her to DIY shops and pick out paints or carry equipment. She kept waiting for the point when he would join in and they would tackle one of the rooms together. And, for a short while, he seemed to be showing more interest, even painted splodges of various shades of grey on the bathroom wall, wrapped up the debate over whether *Grey Owl* was better than *Pale Pewter*.

But then he got his new job – a promotion – and he told her he was too busy to look at screwdrivers, too tired to pick out toilet seats. So that meant not only was she working on the flat alone, but he didn't want to talk or think about the project, either. He was not interested in her trifling achievements, and he no longer congratulated her on what she had done.

Tom became a little more withdrawn, worked longer hours, week by week. In the past, she had been the only one working evenings at home – when she wasn't painting – marking, planning, tracking while he sat on the sofa nearby, watching American sitcoms. But now she worked at home, alone, while he worked in the office, often coming home after nine.

She missed him.

She asked him if he could give up one of his Friday nights out, and spend it with her for a cosy evening in, seeing as they were both so busy. Or they could even go out together. He argued that he had to show his face, had to buy the drinks for his colleagues. That was expected. He was the boss. And besides, now he'd made Financial Director, they could afford to get someone else in to decorate the flat. So she didn't have to feel put upon. There was no need. If she gave that up, perhaps she'd feel better. She could take advantage of the time she was alone, to do something nice for herself, see her sister.

April didn't want to get someone else in. And she didn't think her decorating was the issue, especially as he was rarely there when she did it. She was only doing it for want of a way to pass the time. She marvelled at how it was they had ended up talking about her, and her lifestyle, and how she spent her time, when he was the one who was never there.

She had completely redecorated the kitchen and bathroom, even changing the doors. She had cleaned the carpets in the living room, put some blinds up. Doing their bedroom was all that was left, and she had a vision for it that she wanted to see through. She could do it over the Easter holidays.

That was a difficult couple of weeks. April hadn't factored in that Tom had no time off at all that Easter, bar the long weekend. He went out again with work, on the Thursday this time, and didn't arrive back until 2.30 am. He was quiet for the next two days, claiming a mammoth hangover. They had to cancel plans with family. She had crept around in fear of annoying him. She tried to keep the noise down and be as quiet and tidy as possible while she put wallpaper up and painted the ceiling, though the fumes cut through the air.

She knew he'd be happy when it was done. It would be beautiful. Perhaps it was what they needed: an exquisite bedroom to rest and cuddle up in.

The lack of space to sleep, dress, get ready over the following week, only added to his cranky mood. When he managed to get a small smudge of paint on his navy suit jacket, they had a furious row. He swore, shouted, blamed, and it eventually ended in tears on both sides, and promises to try harder and spend more quality time together. He promised.

But it didn't happen.

The bedroom was finished, Tom carried on exactly the same, and April found herself looking around for other little jobs to do around the house to occupy her time when he continued to work such long hours, or was tired, or out. He was always tense, and she wondered if work was too much for him – but would never dare to say so aloud. It seemed he found her annoying, how she kept on going, kept changing things. His irritation was a fire, always burning, the embers warm, and every day she stoked it with another log: she changed the door knocker; she cut a spyhole in the front door; she fixed a full-length mirror to the bedroom wall; she put up a floating shelf in the living room. To her, it was an accomplishment. To him, it was all simply fuel.

Eventually, he invited her to a black-tie do for his work. April knew the date off by heart for weeks, building this one evening into something special, something that would help to salvage things, and take them back to how they were. They would have a wonderful time. They would laugh and eat and drink. Maybe dance.

She had no idea what to wear at first, and ended up having to get a new dress and buy sparkly sandals when she couldn't find heels that she could walk in. She had always had a problem with shoes. They both dressed up: physically pressed and booted, but emotionally crumpled and tired. It was the first time they'd been out together in months.

When they were seated, April struggled to make conversation with his colleagues and acquaintances. Her work stories revolved around little Jamie's lost trousers after P.E rather than how the office intern had nearly lost them half a million. She felt like someone's little sister; like she'd been asked along by mistake, or out of pity, with her costume jewellery and too-tight Spanx.

It struck her there was a time when they would have been accomplices at these events: saving each other from dire conversations with dribbling, drunken non-executive directors, or giggling behind menus, thick as thieves. But Tom was off working the room and chatting amiably to everyone. It was expected, he said. He had to show his face.

She tried not to mind. She tried hard to be proud of him as he moved confidently about the space, spending an age at table nine where more of his colleagues were. He was a handsome man, his body at ease in his expensive clothes, his smile natural and broad. And he was hers.

Then, at the end of the night, while Tom was queuing for their coats, a young woman appeared at April's side. She was about twenty-eight – maybe younger – and immaculate. April found herself wondering, vaguely, if she'd had her make-up and long, dark hair done professionally, and how long it had taken. She wanted to touch her waves, see if they felt as soft as they looked.

"Hi," the woman said, firmly sticking her hand out for shaking, manicured nails gleaming. "I'm Susie."

April took her hand. "I don't think we've met?" she said.

Susie gave a wan smile. "I love your dress," she said. "Did you manage to find any shoes in the end?"

April was confused. She found herself automatically sliding one foot out from under the table for her to see.

"Ah, OK," Susie said, in a manner that seemed to mean: "That's a shame." April looked down to Susie's shoes, gold-studded with sharp heels three inches high at least.

"You've got quite a catch there. He talks about you all the time."

"Really? What does he say?"

Susie didn't answer. "Has he taken you to that new Japanese place yet? I told him to. Not fair to keep taking me there and not you. That place is wasted on work talk."

"Not yet," April said, tight-lipped. Tom had never been keen on sushi.

"I'm sorry I keep stealing him, but the Longstone Project is taking so much time. Thank God I've got him by my side. I don't know what I'd have done without him."

"Right."

"Have you finished the flat yet? Ready to get it on the market? I'm dying to see it. I'm looking to get a do-er up-er myself —"

"Oh, but it's not really a..." April started to correct her, but Susie was looking away, hardly paying attention.

"Here he comes now," Susie called across the room, "I hope you got me the right coat! Not like last time!"

Susie was laughing, head back a little, straight white teeth exposed. April saw Tom, not laughing, but looking horrified to see them together.

"Oh, you two have met," he muttered. "Talking about anything interesting?"

*

They had not slept together. He promised her that. They had kissed once: OK, no, twice. Both times just a kiss, a long but drunken kiss. Clothes on.

It wasn't an affair.

She was easy to talk to, and yes, he fancied her. Yes, he admitted it. Who wouldn't? And OK, yes, they spent a lot of time together. But much of that was involuntary. What choice did he have? It was her he had been with that Thursday before Easter. She was there every Friday for drinks. There was usually a crowd of them, not just them alone. Usually. Well, yes, they did sometimes go for dinner as well as drinks. Yes. Sometimes on their own. But he did that with

31

other colleagues, sometimes. Maybe not recently, that's just the way it had worked out. But that really doesn't mean anything. He didn't know why he'd never mentioned her.

But April did.

And that was when it all fell apart.

*

Kelly came into the kitchen. "Curtains are up," she said. She was pink in the face. "What's next?"

"Do you want to help me here?"

There was a quiet knock on the flat door.

"I'll get that," Kelly said, apparently keen for an excuse to get away.

April paused in her work but stayed where she was, listening in to hear who this unexpected guest would be. Then she heard voices getting closer.

"Paul was just kind enough to invite us over for coffee," Kelly said, grinning. She was in the doorway of the kitchen, and April could see Paul behind her, clutching a bag of coffee beans.

"I thought you workers could do with a break," he said. "And I'm dying to show off this amazing *Monsoon Malabar*." He was smiling but sounded awkward. Shy, even.

"You're on!" Kelly said.

"Hang on," April answered. "I need to finish these last cupboard doors, remember."

"Dang it," Kelly said. "I was hoping we would get away with that. She's a bloody hard task master, you know."

"So unfair!" April laughed. "I want to get this done. If you two pitch in, it'll be finished in no time. Chop

32

chop, people. Then we can all get to that *Malabar* thingy."

She watched as Kelly wrinkled her nose, and Paul looked surprised – shocked, even.

"I..." he started.

"I'm kidding," April said. "Well, I'm kidding about you helping, Paul." She nudged Kelly in the ribs. "Come on, sis. Get to it."

But it was Paul who was the first to step forward and pick up a piece of sandpaper.

Chapter Six:
Paul

Paul was about to have a week's holiday from work and, as yet, he had made no plans whatsoever. He had a vague idea it might be nice to drive out of town and walk a hill one day, but he hadn't even taken the time to think of which one, or to check the forecast for the best day. That was disappointing, even for him.

He hadn't had time off for over two months, and he was acquiring quite a backlog of days to try to use up in the second half of the year, so he had randomly picked a week's leave and stuck it in the calendar. His colleagues often laughed at him and his ubiquitous presence in the workplace. He was rarely off sick, and was always the first to offer to cover. Last time he was away from work, at Easter, he had been to see an old friend in Bath for a long weekend. They had attempted a beer crawl and listened to some live music. It was uplifting: the only trip out of town he had taken in over a year.

Paul gave himself a shake and decided he'd go to the market to pick up some ingredients to cook himself a celebratory dinner. It wasn't exactly like one of those days of real ale and late-night curries, but still, he couldn't say he craved that. The fresh air would do him good, too. He could drive the scenic route. But it was Sunday, so he'd be cleaning the flat first. To hell with the smells and mess he'd be making afterwards. To hell with it.

He moved efficiently around his home, following his usual routine of working his way around the flat towards the front door and then going straight out. Usually, he parked himself in a café for a while when he finished. There was one nearby that made amazing orange cake and a respectable espresso, and he would sit with a broadsheet paper and take in the sounds and smells of the place, reading and snacking at a leisurely pace. That way, everything in the flat stayed sealed and clean, and the wet floor and surfaces had time to dry while he was out. No chance of dirty feet messing it up.

People thought he loved to clean, but in fact he detested the process itself. He hated the sensation of stickiness, of things that shouldn't be there on his kitchen surfaces, then transferred onto his skin. Plus – something he would hesitate to admit to anyone – he was never completely sure when he should stop. How could you know when something was truly clean? What he did love was the feeling when he returned home later. The hygienic scent, the clear surfaces. It was one of his favourite times of the week.

He was in an upbeat mood, thinking about the forthcoming trip to the market, and the impromptu gathering that had happened recently, outside the house. The boys downstairs had made him laugh, and he had spent a little while chatting to April, discovering she was easy to talk to when she wasn't balancing packing boxes or wrestling with locks. As he had hoped. It was a relief to know he wouldn't be reduced to nodding on staircases again. He could actually have a brief conversation with her.

His bedroom was easy and a great place to start as it was small and square, and he had dressed it in such a way as to be efficient for cleaning. The bed itself was on four legs, not a divan, and he made sure to keep nothing beneath it so he could sweep easily. His huge wardrobe, on the other hand, fit snuggly into the space opposite the bed and left no room for dust to gather above or below it. His chest of drawers was small and fit inside the wardrobe itself, so could be shut away. He only had one bedside cabinet. These things combined meant the space was always spotless, which he had found he needed, if he was ever to get a good night's sleep.

He had finished his bedroom and was taking the dirty washing into the kitchen to put into the washer – that was the next room he'd be tackling so he always took the sheets in once he had finished the bedroom – when someone knocked on his front door. Paul stopped, frozen in the act of shovelling fabric into the machine. Surely this was a mistake. Dai knew not to come at this time, and none of his friends or colleagues would ever turn up unannounced.

There it was again.

Paul wasn't sure what to do but figured it must be important to warrant an unplanned visit, so he pushed the washing in and made his way to the door. It was odd to be moving out of sequence. He had to fight the urge to go back and finish turning on the machine.

He opened the latch to find April standing there.

"Boiler's broken," she said.

Paul stared at her, unclear what the right response should be.

"Oh dear," he said, after a while. He was still holding the latch, with the door only ajar. They were

36

peering through the gap at each other. He noticed her eyes travel to the yellow washing-up gloves he was wearing.

"Bad time?" she asked. She was clearly expecting him to do something, but he was uncertain what.

"I don't know anything about boilers," he replied. "Have you told the agency?"

April gave one hard laugh. "Ha! Of course I did. Seemed a weird thing to be doing when the landlord lives on the premises, but I gather that's the way he likes to run his business, and who am I to judge?"

"I don't think I know what you mean?" he said, still holding the door.

"The landlord. He's... Anyway, I finally tracked down the emergency number, and they tried to put me off until tomorrow. Sunday 'call out' fees and all that. But I wasn't having it and reminded them about the lease and whatnot, and eventually they sent someone round. After a couple of hours of my sitting there waiting, of course. They are there now. My water is off, and it seems like it could be some time."

"Poor you," Paul said vaguely, still peering through the gap, as if they were both in *The Shining*. He knew he probably looked odd, but for some reason he was locked in position.

"I'm not too keen on hanging out there as the bloke who's doing the job isn't the friendliest, and the space isn't all that big. Feels a bit weird to be holed up in there with him... " She'd been talking to the door, the floor, the wall. And now a grin spread across her face, "Oh, you didn't think I was asking you to fix it, did you?"

"No, no, no," Paul said, unconvincingly. "It's just, I'm mid-clean and wouldn't be a very good host to you. And I'm all out of *Monsoon Malabar.*" This was a joke to soften the message. "Have you tried the guys at number one if you're looking for somewhere to, to 'hang out'?" He said it in air quotes, sounding ten years older than he was.

"Tried and failed, my friend," she said. "And no Betty to take me in, either."

They stood in silence for a beat. Then he opened the door a little wider.

"I guess you'd better come inside," he said, reluctantly.

*

He was making coffee when she came back from the bathroom. She had actually started a conversation as she went off and had chatted on loudly while she blew her nose and washed her hands at the sink, even though he was in another room. Even though she was washing herself. For one horrifying moment, it crossed his mind she might go to the toilet with the door open. So he'd come into the kitchen, and her voice dimmed as, presumably, she realised he was no longer there and she was talking to herself.

"You like milk, don't you?" he asked.

"Yes, please."

He noted how she took in the kitchen and glanced away and then back, seemingly trying not to stare for too long, at the large barista-standard machine he was handling. Last time, she'd stayed in the living room.

"Nice," she said, nodding at the machine. "Your kitchen is a hell of a lot better than mine."

"I wouldn't know," Paul said, before thinking perhaps that was not the humblest of responses. "I'm sure you'll make yours lovely," he added.

"Mine is multicoloured and peeling. You've seen it. It's never going to be a show kitchen, even after my best efforts. How come you get the white surfaces? Not fair. You are renting, too, aren't you? Are you their favourite or something?"

"I changed the cupboard doors," he said, as he filled the water reservoir.

"You did?" her eyes widened. "Clever! I do like a bit of home improvement. I completely did up the last place I lived. Not sure I currently have the energy to overhaul this place to the same extent."

He smiled at her. "I have to admit, I paid someone."

She stood and watched him as he made the drinks and put the mugs of coffee and the milk jug onto a tray. "Let's go next door," he said, and carried the tray into the living room.

She stood still for a moment. "You have a tray," she said, sounding surprised.

"Um… indeed I do," he answered, perplexed.

"It seems… I don't know… domesticated."

"If the drinks spill it will go on the tray, not the carpet," he stated.

"Of course, yes," April said, still sounding somewhat confused. She sat on the brown leather armchair and surveyed the room. "I've been meaning to ask when you moved in."

"I don't know. Four years? Five?" Paul answered, passing her a mug.

"Oh! But there's no… there's nothing… there's no *stuff*," she said. "It's completely plain and clean. I thought you'd just moved in."

"Thank you," he answered. This wasn't such a bad

interruption after all.

Chapter Seven:
April

She'd never been to this market before, so arriving to the buzz, the colours, the noise put her in the first genuinely happy mood she'd experienced in months. It actually struck her like that – 'I'm happy.' Then she wondered if she'd cursed it by acknowledging it, as if something horrid was bound to come along to bring her down. Was she acting ridiculously? Perhaps people would think she was odd, smiling and even humming as she walked.

When Paul had mentioned his plans for the day, she immediately said she'd come along, too. She invited herself. In fact, she would be his personal chauffeur, if he'd give directions. He had a strange look on his face, and she wondered if he thought she was mad, or coming on to him, or too damn pushy. But she wasn't any of those things. She was lonely and bored, she had realised with a jolt. And she had time to kill. A market sounded perfect. This was no time to be shy.

April laughed when Paul said he was going to finish cleaning his flat first. He'd miss all the best produce, she said, and cleaning could wait. The place was pristine as it was. She bundled him back into the kitchen and dumped his tray of coffee next to the sink, demanding he leave his rubber gloves and washing up and get a move on. He did as she instructed.

Now they were here, she knew she'd made the right choice. They had struggled to find a space to park, eventually squeezing between two larger cars, testing her parallel parking and power steering. They were a little stretch away from the market but there were throngs of people on the pavement even there. There were children carrying cheap remote-control toys, and men eating hot pies held inside paper bags. They walked along, and she had to make a concerted effort to slow down as she kept finding herself walking two steps ahead of him, racing ahead. Like a child.

"What are you after?" she asked him. "Meat? Clothes? Cheese?"

"Veg, mainly," he frowned.

"Great. I might grab myself some fruit. Lead the way!" she said, so excited she almost grabbed his arm – then realised he would give her one of his startled looks if she did.

He walked past several stands laden with fruit and soft tomatoes, but she said nothing and allowed him to direct them to his preferred stall. Eventually, he came to a smaller pitch with white cloth on the tables. There were baskets made of woven willow and wicker. It was immaculate. He had a warm and easy conversation with the stallholder that showed he was clearly a regular. They discussed various kinds of leafy green veg and examined globe artichokes and fennel as if they were works of art: reverently, with delicate fingers and hushed voices. In the end, he left with several paper bags containing aubergine, chicory, onions, and some kind of peas or beans she didn't recognise.

"So, what's so special about that stall?" she asked

with genuine interest as they walked back through the market.

For a moment he didn't answer, and she wondered if she'd offended him, or perhaps he hadn't heard. She glanced at him, and realised he was considering her question.

"Don't laugh," he said, seriously. "I'm not some sort of hippy, but I like to eat seasonally. That stall is local and organic. I like my food to be pure and not forced, and to eat whatever is in season and fresh that week. It seems somehow right, and respectful. And it makes me eat lots of different things."

"Ah. That makes sense," she said. "I get that."

"Really?" he asked, clearly delighted. "I've never admitted that to anyone before. I thought you might think I was some sort of weirdo." He had stopped walking and was looking at her, beaming.

"Oh, I never said I didn't think you were a weirdo," she teased. "Just not because of that."

*

Later, April felt pleased with herself, cooking up a pot of spinach tagliatelle and stirring through the fresh pesto she had bought from the deli stall. She dropped a mound of their pitted olives on top, sprinkled on some cheese and voila! This was quite possibly the most grown-up meal she had ever made herself. Better than peanuts and lager.

Secretly, she'd been hoping Paul was going to invite her to stay for dinner, because it sounded rather as if he knew what he was doing, but that invite was not forthcoming. He had become increasingly serious as they walked from the car and approached the house, then his flat door. As he put the key in the lock, she saw him briefly close his eyes, and take a breath before opening.

"I'm going to get on with this backlog of cleaning," he said. "Thanks for driving me."

She hardly had time to answer before his door was shut again. Maybe he really was weird. But then, she quite liked a touch of oddity.

April let herself into her flat and wondered if she, too, should be cleaning. But she swiftly rejected the idea. Instead, she had called Kelly and told her about her day and how she planned to rustle up pasta and pesto. Kelly laughed at her enthusiasm, asked her when she'd be getting her dinner party invite. She teased her that her finest hour sounded more pedestrian than exceptional.

"Maybe you could invite that landlord of yours? For some inexplicable reason, an image of him has popped into my mind several times today. Can't think why."

"Don't know that you'd be so keen if you had to spend more than thirty seconds in his company," April said.

"Really? I don't know, that brooding thing he's got going on. Mr Darcy vibes or something."

"He is tolerable looking, I suppose," April joked.

"Hm. Is he rich, do you think?" Kelly asked.

"How should I know?"

"Aren't they always rich, these dark and brooding types?"

"Are they?" April laughed.

"Yup. He owns the house, right? Any more property? Does he work? Or merely go around storming up and down staircases and looking beautiful with a heart full of angst."

"I have no idea about his property investments. But I think he might do something practical, like carpentry or something. I'm speculating. It's just a sense I have. He doesn't wear proper shoes. He looks fit. His doesn't have office hair."

"Office hair? What's office hair? Is that what I have, too?" Kelly laughed. "You're such a snob."

"A snob? I think not."

"An inverted snob," Kelly corrected. "You think anything that's not artistic or in the Public Sector is distasteful."

"Yes, yes. I'm a bohemian. Very funny... You know what I mean. Hair you would be expected to have in an office. He doesn't have it, does he? And he seems to keep odd hours, spends time on his own. I've never seen him in a suit or anything."

"So not Mr Darcy. But Lady Chatterley's lover, maybe? The sexy man in the woodshed?"

"That English Literature degree has given you rather unrealistic ideas of modern men," was all April could think to reply.

Chapter Eight:
April

Hummingbird House seemed to have more than its fair share of jobs and DIY projects on the go most of the time. Perhaps it was the curse of living in an aged property with multiple occupants. A month ago, if you had told her she'd be in an elderly lady's flat, putting together flat-pack bedside cabinets, April would have been bemused, to say the least. And yet here she was. 'One set of drawers down, one to go,' she thought as she tore into the cardboard.

She had bumped into Betty when she was taking some rubbish downstairs. Betty was always friendly, and April had made the mistake of chatting about getting curtains up, and how she was thinking of putting up coat hooks by the door. One thing led to another and the next thing she knew, she had agreed to go to Betty's flat to put her bedside cabinets together. She had seemed to be suitably impressed when April arrived with her own toolkit, which April found rather pleasing.

"Have a cup of tea before you start that second lot," Betty said, as there was a tap on the flat door. "I wonder who that could be?" she said, in a manner that suggested she already knew.

April watched as Betty carefully navigated the short flight of stairs that went up from the basement to the flat door, wondering why she, of all people, occupied this flat, with its dull light and narrow staircase. You'd think the landlord would insist she had a better one. Why hadn't he moved her into number three when he had the chance? At least that flight of stairs was wide enough to put your foot on properly.

It was Dai at the door.

"We're having tea. Do come in, David," Betty said.

"Won't stop," Dai replied, speaking to Betty but looking down at April. She caught his eye, and became conscious of her ratty jeans and ponytailed hair. Why was it she always looked like she'd dressed in the dark when she bumped into him?

She blushed. He looked away.

Betty started walking down the staircase, and he dutifully followed. April watched the unusual duo, both moving stiffly, slowly, and staring down at their feet. There was something comfortable about it. Something sweet, it struck her.

"You're sure you don't want tea, David?"

"No, thanks. Just wanted to say I'll be using, going out… you know… tonight. If you don't mind me out there." He gestured vaguely towards the rear of the property.

Betty waved her hand in the air, floated his deference away. "I've told you before, you can go in that shed any time you like. You don't have to ask me."

"I do. Because it's in your garden."

"No," she said. "*Our* garden. Any time."

"Right. Thanks," he said. There was a moment's silence and then he turned to go. "Bye, Betty. Thanks."

"Bye, David," April said, and chuckled inwardly

when she saw him jump.

Perhaps she was getting back her old self, she realised.

*

That evening, she sat in her little kitchen, with its sanded-but-not-yet-painted cupboards and token blue rug. She was talking to Kelly on the phone while drinking tea. From here, she had a view of several backyards along the terrace. Unlike the uniform and grand exterior at the front, the back of the houses boasted gardens whose boundaries were imperfect and irregular. April found it strangely charming. Hummingbird House had a wider garden than the house to its left, she noted. The wall was at a slight angle, widening greedily as it went, eating into more than its fair share of space.

Some of the other houses had taken large sections of garden away for extensions or more parking, whereas Hummingbird House's garden was mostly lawned, with a wooden table, two benches and chairs to one side. There was an irregular path made up of sunken slabs that led from the back of the house and then forked: one strand towards the shed, and the other to the grass. Along the way were a few potted plants. There were some well-established bushes and flowers in pinks and reds; even one in purple. April admired them, but had no inkling what they were.

She put Kelly on loudspeaker, and started to remove her nail varnish, which had been battered by her earlier handiwork. Kelly was telling her a story about Olive's nursery keyworker shouting at another child, and how she wondered how she was with Olive when there weren't any witnesses. She was anxiously reading aloud the email she had written for the Toddler Room Supervisor. April listened dutifully as she wiped away at her nails. In the end, she advised her she might want to send it straight to the manager, but to sleep on it first. Perhaps a phone call might be better, still. Sometimes it was hard to gauge the tone of an email.

Olive came on the line, and told April how it would be her turn to bring Bonnie Bear home soon, and could she bring her around to the flat so they could take photos? She had to show everyone where Bonnie Bear had been.

"No way! Not Bummy Bear!" April teased. "I don't think I want her anywhere near my house. Phew-ee!"

She could hear Olive's infectious giggle. "Nooo, Aunty April. Not Bummy! Bon-nee."

"Well, that's alright, then. Let's see if we can persuade your mummy to bring you soon, and I'll make you both a little tea party. We can get some really special pictures then."

"Yes, please! Thank you, Aunty April."

She was gone, and Kelly came back on the line, thanking her for coming up with a solution to what they could do with "Bloody Bonnie Bear". As she talked, April moved around the kitchen, taking the used cotton wool over to the bin, flicking her new kettle back on. Glancing out of the window, she stopped Kelly mid-flow.

"What time is it, Kel?"

"Boring you, am I?"

"Sorry, no. But I think my landlord is still out in the shed. He must have been there for bloody hours."

She heard Kelly's voice muffle briefly as she

stretched to see a clock. "Bloody hell, eight-thirty! Olive, you need to get to bed." There were the sounds of voices and little kiddie footsteps running, then Kelly came back on the line. "Sorry. I'll have to go in a sec, but I've sent Russ to start the job off. I had no idea it was —"

"I wonder what on earth he's doing?" April interrupted.

"Who? Russ?"

"My landlord. I saw him go out there when I grabbed a cold drink late afternoon. Four — four-thirty, I suppose. But he's still there."

"Right. Well, God knows. Why does it matter?"

"I don't know. It's just weird," April said, feeling a bit foolish.

"Is it?"

"Yes, the shed is tiny. And it's hot today." The shed was old, wooden and did not look sturdy. The front had double doors, almost like a garage, one of which had dropped down at an angle. The roof was made of cracked black felt.

"He hasn't got a three-year-old he's hiding from, by any chance?" Kelly still sounded distracted, her voice getting louder and then quieter, undulating as she moved and strained, perhaps looking to see how good a job Russ was doing. Or perhaps hiding somewhere. Either scenario was as likely as the other. "Didn't you say he had some practical job? Perhaps he's working."

"Hmm. Maybe."

"How do you even know he's in there?"

"There's a light on."

"Maybe you should ask him?" Kelly was clearly irritated.

"I think I will," April said. "Though not right

50

now."

*

Later, much later, April came to get a glass of water to take to bed. She had discovered the best way to encourage a night's sleep was to wait until she was truly tired, so she had taken to staying up until midnight, at least. That way she could avoid the middle-of-the-night irrational anxiety that had plagued her for the first three or four weeks after she broke up with Tom. There was a period when it escalated into some form of night terror, where she would wake up sweating, to find herself standing by the door having flicked the light switch on, or sat bolt upright in bed, crying out. The longer she stayed in bed, the greater the chance this would happen, she reasoned. Better to be exhausted than panicked.

She stood in the dark of the kitchen and savoured the still, quiet air, punctured only by the harsh light of the fridge as she opened the door to get the jug of water. The cold air washed out and across her bare feet. She moved gently, winding her body down, consciously relaxing as much as she could, trying not to jar herself, or move too quickly, or turn on too many lights. She had to do everything in her power to make friends with sleep or it was elusive, slipping away.

When she closed the fridge and started to move back through the kitchen, she glanced out of the window. The shed light was still on, and the indistinct shadow of a man was moving slowly inside.

Chapter Nine:
Dai

He'd ended up staying in the shed until about two-thirty. There seemed to be a pattern emerging here: what started as the sorting through of boxes inevitably descended into reminiscing, wallowing, then tears. This time, Dai pummelled his emotions into the punch bag, rather than downing a four-pack of lager as he had done last week. He pounded swiftly and repeatedly, until the bag's freestanding frame had shifted and slid across the floor with the force. There was limited room in the shed for him to practise his footwork and movement around the bag. The gym would be far better, for a number of reasons, but he did not think he could face that yet. But this was something at least.

He eventually got to bed at around three, cobwebbed and dewy.

The next day he felt guilty that he had no doubt disturbed Betty with his incessant punching. Everything sounds louder in the early hours. Even the light could have bothered her as the shed was not far from the back of her flat. He was irritated at his own insensitivity. Would she have heard him crying? He reddened at the thought.

At around 11 am, he knocked on the door of her flat to apologise. It was only when she opened that he realised he was still wearing the clothes from the night before.

"Hello, David. How are you?" she said. If she noted his appearance, she was too polite to let it show.

"Did I disturb you?" he asked.

"No, no. I was listening to the wireless, that's all."

"Last night," he clarified. "Did I keep you awake?"

"Not at all. A chamomile tea and a nip of whisky and I am out like a light. Mind you, I'm awake again at five-thirty. That's the curse of old age, I'm afraid. Were you up very late?"

"Yes. Sorry."

"Did you get everything done this time?" she asked, leaning in. He suspected she knew the answer already.

"Not really... I... Well, no. Not at all."

She smiled at him. "David, it'll take time –" she started.

"I feel like I'll never get it done," he said, his voice growing louder, cracking. He cursed her for being so nice to him. He could not cope with empathy.

"My dear boy," she said. "You must come and have a cup of tea."

"And a nip of whisky?" he asked, laughing through the start of tears.

*

Dai sat still and quiet while Betty pottered in the kitchen to the rear. The small flat, with its ticking carriage clock, rag rugs and satin cushions, slowed his breathing until his heart no longer tremored in his chest. There was something very comforting about simply being here. The colours in the room were muted browns and pinks. The place was cluttered but impeccably tidy, and full of personal effects. Oxo the cat wondered into the living room from the direction of her kitchen, clearly at home in the place. He settled himself on a velvet cushion that already had a distinctly cat-shaped indentation in it. Betty made no comment.

He wolfed down the plate of biscuits Betty provided, and drank three cups of tea, before he realised that he could not recall the last time he had eaten. He knew he needed to start looking after himself, pushing himself to make an effort. But he wasn't quite ready. Not yet. He couldn't straighten his thoughts into any semblance of order to enable him to structure his time that way. He couldn't think ahead. It was hard enough to keep track of whether it was morning or afternoon. He could just about manage one-item lists at the moment. One trip out. One meal eaten. Or one box cleared. No more than one; and certainly not all three.

Everything was exhausting.

They chatted about his plans, or at least Betty chatted and questioned, and occasionally he answered. He told her how understanding his work had been about his extended leave, which was one less thing to worry about. He hadn't told anyone else this.

"Unpaid, of course," he said. "But you can't have everything."

It was strange, but true, that he felt comfortable with Betty. He had said more words in her company, in this one meeting, than he had in the past two weeks, and it was demanding, but good. As she talked about a forthcoming trip out with a friend, he started to daydream about a hot shower and a nap. Sleep usually eluded him, but perhaps it would come for once. Perhaps.

"Ah, and I am interested to know, David... what about the new young lady, April? Have you seen much of her?" Betty asked.

He thought back to how she had called him David. The shock he felt in his gut at hearing her use his name. So few people did.

"Not much," he said. "I pass her on the stairs occasionally, that's all. Give her a nod."

"Oh, you can do better than that. You must talk to her. I think she's lovely. A right little firecracker now she's starting to come out of her shell."

Dai shrugged. "At least one of us is able to put flat-pack together."

They sat for a moment, both smiling, relaxed. Then he placed his cup down and brushed his thighs free of biscuit crumbs as he considered getting up to go.

"Before you disappear, there is one little job you could do for me, if you don't mind?"

*

He was on his hands and knees, digging dandelions out of the cracks between the slabs in the front yard. Betty was giving instructions in a firm yet somehow inoffensive manner, pointing out when he had not got the whole root and directing him to the fledgling plants he would have overlooked.

"They are lovely things, really," she was saying. "In their own way. But they don't belong here. They'll take over. Some people call them *Shepherd's Clocks*, you know. Have you heard that?" He simply grunted. She carried on, "Because their flowers open at sunrise and

55

close in the evening. Clever, isn't it? Isn't nature amazing?"

He paused. "We always did that 'Do you like butter?' trick by putting it under our chins." He picked a flower. "Ah, no. That was buttercups. Of course." He felt foolish. He didn't seem able to think straight enough to join in even the simplest of conversations. But Betty didn't seem to note it.

"It's gold, with dandelions. If it glows gold under your chin, you'll grow up to be rich."

"Well, there's more than one way to be wealthy," he said.

He could feel how she watched him, occasionally gesturing with her foot or arm to a spot that needed his attention. He did his best to get it right the first time.

"You should make a wish on one of the seed heads," she said. "It seems rather a waste not to."

"Hello there." Dai heard a woman's voice close behind him and gave a jump. April. He sat back on his haunches and turned slightly to face her, but he did not get up. He hoped she wouldn't notice his dirty clothes and unwashed hair. His three-day-old stubble.

"How do?" he said. *How do?* He had never said that before in his life.

April gave a little "Ha!" sound, as if taken aback, and turned her attention to Betty. "Enjoying the sun?" she asked.

"Oh, yes. My helper is making this trip outside much easier than I thought it would be."

"So I see!" April said. "Oh, I've been meaning to tell you: I tried that tea you recommended, and I love it! I've been sleeping like a log. Relatively speaking, anyway. Compared to before."

56

"I am glad," Betty said.

Dai continued to weed, his back turned to April. He could feel the bottom of his vest had ridden up, exposing part of his lower back. He hoped his underwear wasn't on display.

"Bye, then," April said.

"Goodbye, my love," Betty said.

Dai pretended to be preoccupied with a particularly stubborn dandelion, distracted, holding the stem carefully to try to keep the white fluff whole as he pulled the root from the ground. He heard her walk away, and then a small 'Tsk' from Betty. He raised the seed head close to his mouth and blew.

Chapter Ten:
April

The carpet on the penultimate step of the stairs was lifting. It had worn through, and somehow stretched and rippled, and now a small section had come away completely. It irritated her that she had been forced to report this, a week before, when Dai must have walked on the same step at least twice a day. It was probably his running up and down that had hastened the problem – the man seemed incapable of walking on stairs.

When no one came to sort it out, she took it upon herself to pull and tack the carpet back herself. Better safe than sorry.

Paul came out of his flat, no doubt attracted by the banging. She looked up. He was dressed in his usual navy trousers and a checked shirt. She noted his slightly worn, brown slippers.

He raised his eyebrows. "Moonlighting as a handyman?" he asked.

"Someone has to," she answered gruffly, hammering in a tack. Her hands were sticky and warm.

"Do you want a hand?"

"Shouldn't you be at work?" she asked, realising, as she said it, how unfriendly she sounded.

"Holiday," he said, looking strangely sheepish.

"Well… thanks, but I'm almost finished. And it's

not how you should be spending your holiday. Not really you who should be helping at all. Or me. Either of us. It's bloody annoying," she muttered. She knew she was being irritable.

"The agency isn't the quickest in sending people out if they don't think it's an emergency. The extractor fan has been playing up in my bathroom for months and they keep saying they'll sort it, but…" He had come over to where she was, and squatted down close her, awkwardly.

"Yes, but you'd think the dude upstairs would have done it himself. Too busy storming up and down in trackies that don't fit properly." April had seen him again that morning. She was annoyed with herself for not saying anything about the step.

Paul passed her another tack. "Dai? He's not the best at this sort of thing. But he's a good fella when you get to know him."

April looked up and scrunched her nose. "If you say so." Then she went back to banging.

Paul stood. "Yes," he said, flatly. "Actually, I do." He walked back to his door. "You seem to have this sorted, but give me a knock if you need a hand. Bye, April."

His door banged shut.

*

"And then he just walked off. Practically slammed the door in my face."

"He slammed the door?"

"OK, not exactly. But he definitely huffed off pretty quickly," April corrected.

"Wow," was all Kelly said.

"Can you believe that?"

"I guess. I don't know." Kelly sounded distant.

"You OK?" April asked. "This a bad time?"

"No, not at all. I'm on my own for once, actually."

"Oh… so, yeah. Can you believe that?"

Kelly paused. "Listen, you're not going to like this, but I don't blame him. You don't know the bloke. He doesn't need your moods, or your earfuls."

"I wouldn't exactly call it an earful —"

"Either of them. You don't know either of them. It's not like your landlord's a notorious mass murderer or anything. It's not exactly nice to be slagging him off like that. You've become very critical. You hardly know him."

"Hah!" April spat. "*Nice*? Why am I expected to be nice?" She was taken aback.

"Why not?" Kelly said. "You used to be nice to everyone."

"Look where that got me," April mumbled.

"I met him, and he was a bit off, yes. Not friendly. But so what?" Kelly asked. "He doesn't have to bend over backwards to befriend you. Maybe he's shy. You don't have to be mean."

"Mean?"

"Listen, you asked me, and I'm telling you. I've noticed recently you seem more upbeat, more sort of… confident, I guess? But also, a bit snappy. About him, at least. You never used to be judgemental. Anyway, it's something to be aware of." There was a moment's silence on the phone before Kelly added, "Sorry."

"Judgemental! Wow. OK." That was the opposite of how April had always thought of herself. Of everyone in the family, she'd always been the one with a soft spot for oddballs and eccentrics; always the one with patience. "I don't really know what to say to that."

"Like I said, I'm sorry if that is upsetting. But I thought you'd want to know."

"Is that an 'I'm only saying this because I love you' sort of line?" April said, with a slightly bitter edge.

"Something like that. And you do know I love you. Plus, I think you fancy him," Kelly said.

This change of tack shifted the tone of the conversation and April was happy for the respite. "Dai? Actually no," she said, truthfully. "I did, yes. Briefly. When I first saw him. In a 'I can't believe he's so stunning' sort of way. I mean, he's gorgeous, right? Striking. But I don't fancy him now. I've seen him around a few times and, honestly, no. I don't fancy him. He's rude. And he seems arrogant." She heard Kelly sigh. "But – OK- I will try to give him a chance. I'll try not to be so quick to judge."

"Arrogant can be sexy. Are you sure you don't like him, just a bit?"

"Yes."

"What is it, then?" Kelly asked.

"I think... I don't want to let anyone treat me like crap anymore. I want to stand up for myself, I suppose. He doesn't even say hello to me, sometimes. Two days ago, I held the front door open for him and he barely nodded his thanks. There's no need for it. Manners cost nothing."

"OK. But can't you ignore it? He does seem to get under your skin," Kelly said.

"I don't want to ignore it. Looking back now, I wince when I think of how short Tom was with me towards the end. And Dai is much the same, the way

61

he grunts and doesn't even form full sentences... with Tom, I was so desperate to make it work. You know he started swearing at me? And I let it go."

"Swearing at you? What do you mean?" April could hear Kelly's breath down the line, as she clearly clutched the phone tighter.

"I don't mean abusive. It wouldn't be fair to say that. But he would mutter under his breath if I did something. In the end, he didn't even really try to hide it. That's how little he thought of me. Or if he thought I'd done something, or wanted to blame me, he'd mutter insults. I know now he was only taking it out on me. Or perhaps he was trying to push me away – push me to leave. It's almost embarrassing to admit. And I didn't think anything of it then because I got used to it. Can you believe that? I was used to it. But I do now. I do think something of it. So, I feel I need to stand up. This is me, standing up for myself."

"That makes sense," Kelly said. "But maybe you are standing up to the wrong guy. Dai isn't Tom."

*

She'd had to park her car on the other side of the road, a short walk from Hummingbird House. It wouldn't usually bother her, but of course this would be the day when she had done a huge supermarket shop and had a boot full of fresh pasta, bottled beer, fruit, and pizzas.

Gung-ho for some reason, she decided it was preferable to attempt a military expedition and do the trip in one go. She overloaded herself, with bags cutting her palms and uncooperative pears attempting to break free. Glad to make it home, sweaty, and vaguely embarrassed to have been spotted by the odd pedestrian along the way, she rested a bundle of bags on the floor by her feet at the front door. They settled around her shoes in a heap. She had a baguette under one arm and was shaking her handbag with the other, trying to retrieve her door key, when she heard a woman calling.

"April! I didn't know you lived here."

She swung around to see a familiar figure on the pavement a few metres away. It was Rosie. She dropped the baguette and hopped over the shopping towards her.

"I can't believe it! Long time no see," April cried.

Rosie had been a part-time art teacher at school, coming in three times a week to deliver messy and expressive sessions that seemed to involve an awful lot of walking around the room to music or exploring the school garden. She'd moved on a little under a year ago and was sorely missed.

They hugged. "You're living here, then? Hummingbird House?"

"Yes, been here almost a month now."

"Fab," Rosie said. "Still at the school?"

"Uh-huh. Counting down the days until the start of term," April said, pretending to shudder.

"Just you here?" Rosie gestured to the house; she had always been direct.

"Just me," April said. "Thank God. Come in for a cuppa?"

*

Rosie told April stories: about an art exhibition where one of the other exhibitors had gotten drunk and

63

turned up in smoking jacket and underpants; of how she'd booked a holiday to Morocco but not made it, so now she was considering Laos instead; about how she'd spent a month trying to eat nothing but raw fruit and vegetables and made herself ill; and how she'd recently rescued a hedgehog from this very street.

She was a kaleidoscopic talker: colourful, fast, almost unbelievable in her tales. It was captivating and tiring at the same time. April felt she was inside a bubble of intimacy when she spoke to Rosie – an honoured confidante. And yet, they hadn't spoken in at least four months. So perhaps she made everyone feel that way.

She was an unusual person. One might assume she was fluffy, or weak, or ditsy, based on her interests and style, but the truth was she was hyper-organised and sharp. April could see her assimilating facts and insights based on the little she had given away about her break-up with Tom, until she came out and asked her directly exactly what had happened.

April skirted over the full story, avoiding the details about Susie and Tom's moods, but was pleased to find, for the first time, she was able to explain it without welling up. It may have been the abridged version, but this was an achievement, nonetheless.

"So, you could think about going for a promotion or a new role now. Nothing holding you back," Rosie said, looking down into her peppermint tea.

April was surprised. "I guess so. Though there wasn't ever anything *holding me back* before. I just never really thought about it."

"I don't know about that," Rosie said. "We chatted about the Head of Key Stage job, remember? I know you liked the sound of it. And you would have been a shoo-in for that dyslexia role. They even hinted you should apply. I've always told you you'd be a great manager."

April laughed. "Have you?"

"Don't you remember? I do. I told you lots of times. Because I meant it. You've got so much potential. You've got both the passion and the brains, and that's what a school needs. It's rare. But it seemed to me you were always too worried about..." she trailed off.

"I don't know if it's as simple as that. I don't want to paint Tom as some old sexist pig who didn't want his lady to get promoted —"

"I didn't mean —" Rosie began.

But April waved her apology away and ploughed on. "But you might be right in some respects. About the timing, I mean. Maybe it was me holding myself back, or something. I had other things on my mind. Other priorities. Perhaps now is the time to start thinking about a change. Once the sale of our old flat goes through, maybe. Maybe I will. Who knows?"

"He's not keeping it?"

"No. Not cool enough, not close enough to work." 'Or to Susie, no doubt,' she thought. A small tremor ran through her. But she did not cry. She would not cry.

"And not cool enough for you, either?" Rosie teased.

"Possibly too cool, actually. I am starting to think I am happier in this neck of the woods... But besides that, too many memories," she said. "It was meant to be a flat for two. I didn't want to stay there on my own, looking at an empty chair across the dining table."

"I can certainly understand that."

Almost two hours had gone by before they finished catching up, and April's shopping still sat in a pile of plastic bags and condensation.

"You must come round for dinner," Rosie said, as they hugged goodbye. "I don't want to lose touch with you again." She was earnest, enthusiastic. "And I'm so close!"

April smiled, and scribbled her phone number on a scrap of paper. "You can message me — or just bang the door, I guess."

She didn't really think much would come of it until she received a text the next day:

Free this Friday at 7.30? I bumped into your gorgeous neighbour and we hatched a plan. Come to mine? xxx

Chapter Eleven:
Paul

He had only gone to buy windfall apples, and somehow, by the end of the conversation, he'd agreed to attend a dinner party with Rosie and her housemate.

She often had garden fruit or vegetables on sale for pin money in a basket outside her house, three doors down. There was something very charming about the honesty box, and the signage she'd painted on a row of smooth stones. The box was made from a converted wooden crate, turned sideways, decorated, and weighted. He'd bought her produce plenty of times before – wonky carrots or overgrown courgettes – and he had gotten over his initial qualms about where they had been by having a good chat with Rosie a few months ago. He'd realised she did actually know what she was talking about, and that she had already given all the produce a cursory rinse. And it was super-fresh and seasonal, so worth it. Nothing could be more local.

As he came out of Hummingbird House, he spotted there was a new crop of apples and decided to check it out straight away, to get his pick. They were thick-skinned and rough, but large and fresh. He loved the irregular sizing and shapes of them; their feel in his hands. He was carefully placing them into one of the paper bags provided when Rosie came out.

Barefoot. Not even any slippers.

"My dear friend," she said. "I wondered how long it would take you to spot these beauties! Take as many as you want. Don't worry about giving me the right money: I need shot of them. I swear I have crumble pumping in my veins at the moment."

Paul smiled. "I can't resist a bargain. I was thinking apple sauce. I can bring you some, too, if you'd like?" This little spontaneous flourish took even him by surprise.

"Apple sauce…" Rosie smiled. Rosie looked away and then suddenly leant forward with a conspiratorial grin. "I tell you what: bring some round on Friday and I'll cook you dinner! I have a friend who I hope will come over, and Joy will be here, too. You know Joy?"

He nodded. He did know Joy: she was stunning, with her striking bleached afro – who could miss her? But he wasn't sure if she was a lodger, a housemate, or something else altogether.

"You must come. Now, what goes well with apple sauce? Goats' cheese, maybe? Or a cheese board. Oo… savoury scones!"

He hadn't actually said he was coming but it seemed like a done deal.

"Shall I bring anything else?" he asked, accepting his fate.

"No, no… except wine, of course." She patted him on the arm as he reached with his coins into the moneybox.

"Seven-thirty?"

*

So now here he was, standing in his kitchen, cooking

up Bramley apples and debating whether to keep the sauce plain, or spice it with ginger. Perhaps half each? When he was younger, he would not have imagined this was the way he would be spending his holidays from work. It wasn't exactly rock 'n' roll.

Still, would he want it any other way?

He sniffed the steam above the pan and tried to commit this moment to memory. It was a habit he had. His aunt had once told him your sense of smell has the strongest link to recall. He was certain she was right.

Paul's memories all revolved around food. The first time he saw Father Christmas he still had half a shortbread man in his hand. He could remember how the crumbs started congealing on his fingers, and how he didn't want to put the biscuit down – in case he never got it back – but how the sensation was both fascinating and disgusting. It started as gunk and slowly turned gritty as wet sand. He was more interested in staring at his fingers than at Santa: the picture on his mum's mantelpiece was testament to that.

When he was eight, they went out of the county to a spectacular firework display for Bonfire Night. The November air was sharp and fresh, and the scent of hotdogs and popcorn cut through, warm and strong. He wore wellingtons and an itchy hat. He had chips in a cone, with cheap sweet ketchup and too much vinegar. He took so long to eat them the little wooden fork became slightly soggy: acrid, pungent. His parents had been frustrated with how slowly he walked as he ate, and how little attention he paid to the Guy Fawkes figure as it burned. They thought it spoiled evening. They were wrong.

At the age of twelve, they went on holiday abroad for the first time. The airline lunch was a foil-wrapped disaster, but the sights and smells of Greece, when they arrived, astounded him. Lemon. Fish. Courgettes. Lamb. Thick tomato stews. Oily aubergine dips. Flaked pastry parcels, sweet and savoury. He ate it all, much to the amazement of his parents, who looked on with a heady mix of admiration and horror, while ordering ham and eggs.

That was, even now, his favourite holiday ever.

Aged sixteen, he left school and went to the local college to train in Culinary Arts. The arancini he was served at the open evening had sealed the deal for him, even though his parents begged him to do A Levels or Business Studies. He had not regretted it. He'd been consistently top of the class.

The first meal he ever cooked for Jennifer was arancini. He tried a new recipe with prawns and could still recall the squidge of them inside the crisp shell of the rice ball. She didn't like seafood, it transpired.

And then, when they broke up – he'd been twenty-eight – he stopped cooking, and changed his job altogether.

Chapter Twelve:
April

Kelly had taken the week off work to spend time with Olive, so the pair of them came to have the promised tea party with Bonnie Bear. April had been to a charity shop the afternoon before, on a whim, and bought some old china plates and cups. She had enjoyed rummaging amongst the crockery and picking out an array of contrasting patterns and colours. She had set up a picnic-cum-dining table on the floor and placed fairy lights around the cutlery. She even put blackcurrant squash in her teapot. She was rather pleased with her little display. Olive's mouth dropped open, and she took two steps back in shock when she saw the scene. She clasped her hands together in excitement.

They ate tiny cucumber sandwiches and enjoyed posing the bear in various, increasingly ridiculous, positions while Kelly played photographer and barked instructions. By the time the bear had ended up with a doily skirt and one leg covered in whipped cream, they realised they should call it a day.

After a quick (and somewhat basic) tidy up, Kelly produced a colouring book and a pack of stickers from her giant 'mum satchel' and Olive settled on the duvet beanbag that still held pride of place as a second seat in the living room. Kelly took the armchair and yanked the beanbag towards her seat, and April sat, cross-legged, on the wooden floor. The two women each held a hot coffee.

"Not as good as what's-'is-name's, is it?" Kelly said, absently, as she pushed Olive's hair away from her face.

"Eh?" asked April.

"Coffee."

"Paul's? No, but I get the impression he's a bit of a connoisseur."

"Can you be a coffee connoisseur?" Kelly wondered, vaguely.

"If you can, he is one. He's an everything connoisseur. Food-wise, anyway."

Kelly smiled. "It's nice you've got some good people around you."

"Yup. I think I can... I can actually feel myself starting to relax. I'm sleeping better than I have in months. Not brilliantly, but better. I take that to be a good sign."

"You said," Kelly nodded. "Perhaps you could rub some of that magic off on Olive?" She yawned. "So, will you stay here when the flat sells, do you think? Or are you keen to buy your own place?"

April dropped her head back against the seat of the sofa behind her. "Ugh. The thought of bloody moving again. All that mess. And hassle. I don't think I can face it."

She thought back to the time spent dividing up her possessions and boxing things away. It wouldn't be the same, of course, without the bleak, black heartbreak, but having only lately taken everything out of newspaper and bubble wrap, she dreaded the idea of doing it over again so soon.

"I can understand that. There's no rush. And who knows when all the logistics will be sorted out, anyway? It could be a while before the cash comes through."

"What little of it there is."

"We'll see," Kelly said, with her fingers crossed in front of her face.

*

When they came back from the kitchen, having done the last of the dishes and wrapped the remaining food in cling-film, they found that Olive had nodded off on the beanbag duvet. She was curled into a ball like a kitten, Bonnie Bear under one arm and a thumb wedged into her mouth. At first, April was alarmed, worrying this might mean an even worse night's sleep for her sister, but Kelly reassured her this nap was long overdue.

"Either she needed a nap, or I did, and I'd rather it was her. We can't both go around overtired and cranky, or heads could roll. I'll leave her another twenty minutes or so before I move her." She took her phone out of her bag and snapped a couple of pictures. "She looks so serene."

"More coffee?" April asked.

"I guess I need it if she's going to be up late. But I don't want to wreck your kitchen after we have just sorted it…" she tailed off.

"My kitchen is usually wrecked."

They tiptoed back to refill the cafetiere and stood in the peeling paint of the kitchen. April told Kelly about bumping into Rosie, and the invitation to dinner. Kelly said she thought she had vague recollections of Rosie from a birthday party a couple of years ago.

"It was lovely to see her, but now it's going to turn into *Gardener's Bloody Question Time* or something." She gestured to the ceiling.

"What *are* you talking about?" Kelly asked.

"Mr Personality —" She stopped herself. "Sorry, Dai, I mean. She's invited him."

"He's a gardener, then?" Kelly ignored the insult.

"Something like that. He was pulling up weeds for Betty Williams the other day, and he certainly looked the part." She gestured downstairs. "He was examining them in great bloody detail, nose practically on the ground."

"And you have something against gardeners because…?" Kelly left the question hanging so that its absurdity filled the space between them.

"Look, it's not what he does. I don't care. He's just so difficult to talk to. Rosie is the opposite. It will change things."

Kelly held her mug to her lips and blew on the hot coffee, avoiding eye contact.

April persisted. "I take on board what you said, I really do. But the man is hard work. I hope he's not going to put a dampener on the evening. I fancy having a bit of a blow-out. It's about time."

"So don't go snogging him," Kelly said, quietly, wiggling her eyebrows.

April laughed, surprised. "As if I would!"

*

Half an hour later, April followed her sister down the stairs to the front door, carrying her bag for her and a bundle of left-over sandwiches. Olive was awake, but glassy-eyed and floppy, resting her chin on her mum's shoulder as she carried her cautiously down the stairs.

"You'll be getting too big for this soon, missy," Kelly said.

Jonty was on his way out of the front door and paused when he saw them coming down the steps, standing to one side to hold the door open for them. When they reached the bottom of the stairs, they crowded into the small lobby space together as he admired Olive and complimented Bonnie Bear, who hung limply from Olive's hand. She didn't reply, burying her face into her mum's hair as a signal that she didn't want to converse. Jonty simply laughed.

"Ignore my darling daughter," Kelly smiled. "She's uncharacteristically quiet when she meets strangers."

"I'm equally anti-social when I've just woken up," April said, stroking the top of Olive's head. "Hopefully see you both soon. It's been wonderful to catch up."

Luckily, Kelly's car was parked right outside Hummingbird House, so she was loaded up and off in no time. Olive hardly stirred, and April wondered again about Kelly's chances for later. Jonty stayed in the yard, patiently propping the door open with one foot.

"I wasn't sure if you had a key, my dear."

"Oops. Sorry to hold you up. I didn't think."

He smiled. "No problem at all. And how are you settling in? It's an unusual place this. I have friends who have never even seen their neighbours, but we're like a sort of dysfunctional family, in a way. Well, maybe that's overstating it, but I'm sure you know what I mean."

"I don't know about dysfunctional; I am glad of it. I think it's made life easier for me. Though some of you are more friendly than others," she said.

He glossed over that. "We haven't had one of our famous barbecues in a while. That will be fun! You have to come. House rules."

"You're on. I'll bring the ketchup," she said. He looked bemused. "I'm not exactly known for my cooking," she clarified.

"Wait until you try Betty's strawberry shortcake. I put on half a stone last summer, just looking at it. She is one impressive woman. I hope I'm still in the game when I'm her age."

April wasn't sure exactly what he meant, but chuckled anyway as she walked past him and back up the stairs to her flat, thinking of barbecues and dinner parties.

Chapter Thirteen:
April

Now that it was Friday, she felt a growing panic at the thought of socialising with people she did not know very well. Rosie was lovely, of course, but April was not in the habit of talking to her at length – only occasionally – and had only ever met up with her outside of work en-masse, with other staff. She felt irritated she'd used up all her best anecdotes and news over their coffee earlier in the week. She was wracking her brain to think of some fluffy little stories to relay, but all that came to mind was the flat move and cardboard boxes.

It was the first time she had been out properly since her break up with Tom, which meant it was the first time she had been out as a singleton. It wasn't any fear of flirting or romance that hit her, rather the lack of another half to be the funny one or to answer questions when she was stuck. She always thought it was much easier to socialise as half of a couple. You could bask in the glow of their social skills and hope everyone associated those skills with you, also. It was as if you only needed to contribute half as much, independently. Was this a sign of low esteem, or of lack of identity? She wasn't sure, and decided to leave that box firmly shut for now, instead doubling down on her efforts to think of some witty tales.

She had woken early and forced herself to stay in bed for a while, reading and then playing with her phone with the excuse of 'window shopping' online for some new work clothes. She had itchy feet by around ten, and made herself coffee and then showered in the rattly bathroom. By late morning, she could feel her anxiety rising, and she had decided to go out, but avoiding the traffic by getting the bus to the out-of-town shopping centre.

She found herself wandering around the supermarket, unsure of what was an appropriate little gift to take – chocolates? Flowers? Neither seemed right for Rosie. She also had a pang of doubt about her choice of wine, even though this was one area of grocery shopping where she usually excelled. In the end, she settled on a Pouilly-Fumé and a small orchid and marched herself back home on foot instead of taking the bus again as she had planned.

She arrived home hot and sweaty, but with a clearer head. She decided her best course of action was first to spend much longer than usual getting ready, so as not to feel pressure or rushed and – hopefully - to look her best. Second, she would wear something comfortable and well-loved. Third, she would have a gin and tonic before she went. Fourth, she would drink, but not get too drunk, tonight. It wasn't the most complex of master plans, but it was the best she could do.

By two o'clock she had picked out and even ironed her outfit – the first time the iron had been out since she moved in – and by three-thirty she'd showered, again, and was now blow-drying and straightening her usually wayward, wavy hair.

Feeling a bit more presentable, around four-fifteen

she settled down at her little kitchen table with a cup of chamomile tea and tidied her nails, even painting them with a coat of clear nail polish. She didn't risk painting a colour, for fear of smudges and stress. It was too early to dress and do her makeup, so she had set up a book in front of her, in a pretence of relaxing, but she could not focus.

She stared idly out of the window and noticed Betty and Dai in the back garden, standing by the tatty shed. They seemed to be having a heated conversation. Betty stood with her back to her, straight and neat, while Dai went through a series of large, uncoordinated movements as she talked, his face inscrutable; first he stood with his arms folded, next he threw them wide in the air, and then he burrowed his fingers into his eye sockets as he held his head in his hands.

April watched, mesmerised, wondering what they could be talking about to bring out such strong emotions – at least, in one of them. There was a moment of stillness until he pulled his hands away again and turned brusquely from Betty as if to go into the shed. But he only made it two steps before he stopped.

For a moment, April considered whether she should go down to Betty, to help her deal with this peculiar and difficult man. It seemed extraordinarily inappropriate that he should be acting this way with an elderly lady. Bullish. But she hesitated, thinking of the scene when they had come down Betty's stairs together, and how she called him David, and how he had weeded for her. She obviously knew him better than April did. Perhaps April's presence would make things worse.

And then she was pulled out of her thoughts again, amazed by the scene as it unfolded before her. Betty moved towards him, reaching up to gently hold his broad shoulders. Rather than railing against her, as April expected, Dai seemed to crumble at her touch. He turned towards her and fell into her delicate arms as she embraced him. They rocked together, hugging in the warm sun of the back garden. His thick dark hair contrasted harshly with hers, pale and fine; this large, muscular young man, comforted and patted by a bird-like elderly lady.

April moved into the living room, painfully aware of how she was intruding on an intimate, personal scene.

*

She had chosen her denim skirt, and a white cotton blouse. The skirt was her go-to, and the blouse was at least five years old, but she loved the broderie anglaise on the edging and the way it tied under her bust, hiding her tummy. She picked out a cheerful knitted cardigan, multicoloured, a little newer, to wear with it. Then she selected some pretty, slip-on ballet flats. Not sandals. She even clipped her hair up, allowing a few strands to fall down around her face, and adding long, silver earrings. She wore mascara and blusher, and her legs were shaved. This was the most effort she had made in months. So, when she looked in the mirror, she was reasonably content.

At seven-twenty, she grabbed the wine from the fridge and carefully placed the plant in its paper gift bag. She figured that Dai was the type to arrive late to things, and she wanted to be in there ahead of him.

Then it would be her territory, with him on the hop, rather than vice versa. She downed the last of her gin and tonic, and made her way out of the flat, quietly, praying not to bump into him.

Rosie lived three doors down, in Number Eighteen, but April hadn't yet been inside. Number Eighteen had a parking space outside the front window, currently taken up by an old-style Mini, and it had a cheery pillar-box red front door. But other than that, it looked almost the same as Hummingbird House.

She knew Rosie was on the ground floor. As she approached the house, she discovered its conversion was quite different from Hummingbird House, and any similarities were lost once you ventured inside. The front door was open and there was another, internal, door at the foot of the stairs. There was no corridor in Number Eighteen. April stood in a very small entranceway with one door immediately in front of her, and another to her right, which was presumably the entrance to Rosie's. It was disorientating not to see the same beige carpet and Betty's door tucked away at the end of a small corridor. April wondered how they accessed the basement flat.

She had to ring the bell and knock several times on Rosie's door before she was heard. Laughter and music swelled up as the door opened. She was greeted enthusiastically by a stunning black woman with a tight blonde afro, wearing turquoise eye shadow and a short, mustard-yellow dress. April immediately felt underdressed.

"You must be April!" the woman cried, throwing her arms around her. "Come in, come in. Rosie is making some rather dangerous-looking cocktails in the kitchen… Well, she *says* it's a cocktail, but really I think she's looking for an excuse to use up the rum." April's self-consciousness was diminished by this genuine welcome. "I'm Joy, by the way!"

"Don't listen to a word she says," Rosie called out from the kitchen.

There was music playing, which sounded Cuban, perhaps. The flat was a jumble of objects and plants, but immaculately kept, with brocade, and throws, and various shades of wooden furniture. April wasn't sure where to look, as her eyes were drawn to all the treasures and colours around her.

They walked to the back where the kitchen was, and April proffered her wine and the orchid, which Joy greeted with rapturous noises.

"I hope you like red chillies," Rosie said.

"I love them."

"It's a good job. You don't have much choice in this house," said Joy.

Rosie pretended to flick her with the tea-towel she was holding. "You love it as much as I do," she laughed. "Mai Tai?" she asked April.

"Of course!"

"I mean, it's as close to a Mai Tai as I could make it. I didn't have any orange liquor, so I put in a splash of fresh orange and some extra dark rum for good measure."

Joy's eyes widened. She was eyeballing April and gesticulating at Rosie, emphatically pointing with both hands, clearly very tickled by this revelation. "See! I told you, April. Me girl here saying not to listen to me, but I told you the truth. You'd best watch your drinks tonight. She's heavy-handed."

Rosie passed April her glass, which was chunky and

large, in aqua-blue glass. All the three of them raised their glasses together in a toast. Three different shaped and coloured glasses, in three very different hands.

"Cheers!" she said, laughing.

This was going to be a good night.

And then the doorbell rang.

For that brief moment, she had forgotten they weren't eating alone, and her heart sank at the thought of Dai with his peculiar mannerisms and gruff voice. These few minutes of girls together had reminded her how wonderful women's company could be. She wondered what had possessed Rosie to invite him.

"I'll get it!" Rosie cried, taking a big swig before putting her glass back down.

"Sit. Sit," Joy said to April. "We'll hang out in here for a while. I love the kitchen, don't you? It's the heart of the house."

Joy was pumping her with questions and already topping up her glass when Rosie came back. She could hear her calling over the music, explaining how the front of the house was the dining room, not a bedroom. Things were back to front here.

"I'll show you around in a bit," she was saying. "But you need a drink first."

Rosie walked into the kitchen and straight to a cupboard to find a glass for Dai. Except it wasn't Dai, it was Paul.

"Hi!" April said. "I didn't expect to see you here."

"Didn't you?" he replied, confused, looking to Rosie for an explanation.

"I told you, April," was all she said as she started to fill his glass.

"No, I knew Dai was coming, but I didn't know about Paul. I mean, it's nice to see you, obviously."

"Who's Dai?" Rosie said, looking at her, perplexed. "It's just us four, missus. You've got your wires crossed. We're all here."

"But you said..." April trailed off, realising just in time how tactless it would be to explain why Rosie's text had confused her: *'Your gorgeous neighbour.'* She looked again at Paul smiling bashfully at Rosie while she and Joy admired the two jars of chutney that he had given to them. She was very glad to learn she had been mistaken.

After the jug of Mai Tai was finished and the album came to an end, Rosie took Paul and April for a tour of the flat. She didn't imagine there would be much to see, but, as it turned out, it was much bigger than the ground floor flat in Hummingbird House. Their place consumed the whole of the ground floor, including the corridor space, and also what would be the equivalent of Betty's basement flat. A door in the kitchen took them downstairs to where they had a second bathroom, a large bedroom, and a utility area. It was closer to a maisonette than anything else. They had bought it two years ago. Every room was packed with greenery: herbs in the kitchen, even a propagator next to the tumble dryer.

"How do you manage your cleaning?" Paul asked. "It must be a lot of work with all these..." He struggled to find the right word, "Shelves."

April grinned, thinking back to the vision of him in rubber gloves on the day her boiler had broken down. They should take a trip to the market again sometime, she thought.

"It's ready!" called Joy, and they all trudged back upstairs.

*

The starters were quesadillas with sweetcorn, chilli, and lime – with organic chicken for those who wanted it, and tofu for those who didn't. April had one of each. There was salad, and mashed avocado, and homemade salsa. The chilli was from a huge plant, spreading and wrapping around sticks to scaffold it, in the dining room window. The lettuce came from the garden, the tomatoes from plants on the kitchen windowsill.

"Not exactly haute cuisine, Paul, sorry," Rosie said, scrunching her eyebrows together.

"Oh, I don't know, this is right up your street, isn't it?" April nudged him with her elbow. "Super fresh."

"Mm…" Paul said, nodding briskly, mouth full of food.

"I think he likes it!" April said.

Paul smothered a laugh and made a show of finishing chewing and swallowing. "How can you tell?" he joked. "Delicious!"

"Rosie was a bit worried about cooking for a chef, but I told her not to stress, because everything she makes ends up being amazing, even when she simply shoves random things in the pan… as she usually does," Joy said.

Rosie smiled at her affectionately, and wrinkled her nose. "Don't give away all my secrets at once."

"You're a chef?" April turned to Paul, surprised.

"Isn't it obvious?" said Rosie.

"Correction. I *was* a chef," he said. "A few years back."

April tried to picture him in a hot kitchen, barking orders amidst fragrant, and not so fragrant, steam.

Food stains. Stress. Teamwork.

"Oo… this is interesting. You two can get to know each other's little secrets here tonight. Paul, April is a primary school teacher. And a very talented one, at that," Rosie said.

"Yes, I knew she was a teacher," he smiled, placidly. April reddened, realising he had asked her all about herself, but she had made little effort to get to know him. "What did you think I did?" he asked. "What would you have guessed, if you didn't know I was a trained chef?"

"I… well, I don't know." She was unsure whether her answers would cause offence.

"Yes… What do you think he does now?" Rosie asked, her tone loaded.

"Oh! I know! I know!" Joy said.

They were all enjoying her discomfort, she gathered.

"Quiet you, no cheating. I already told you. I want to know what April's guess would be."

"A… An… Oh, this is really stressful. A fireman?" April laughed. "An astronaut?"

"A bouncer?" Rosie quipped.

"Really," he said, suddenly a touch more serious. "What is your impression of me, April? What do you think I do for a living? I want to know."

"An accountant?" she asked, quietly.

He guffawed until he coughed and had to take a large swig of water.

"That's hilarious," he said, patting her hand briefly.

The main course was an array of different foods, a mini buffet of sorts. Red cabbage with apples from the garden; red onion tart; cold cooked meats; asparagus frittata; new potatoes and heaps more salad.

86

April was amazed. "This is phenomenal, Rosie. How did you find the time?"

Joy cleared her throat, pointedly.

"The frittata is made by my beautiful sous chef, who also scrubbed the potatoes, and I will admit I made the tart yesterday. The rest of it was easy."

As they ate, April discovered Paul, in fact, worked for a charity with homeless adults, in a management role. He had started as a Team Leader for the support staff, when he decided the culinary world wasn't for him anymore. He did that for about eighteen months until a more senior post came up and he was promoted. He spoke with passion about his role and the organisation.

"Do you miss working directly with the homeless people?" she asked.

"It's a charity. There's not really a hierarchy. I still end up spending a fair bit of time 'out front' with the clients. We're all a team."

April considered how different he looked when he talked about this world: how his eyes danced, how he spoke through an irrepressible grin about the difference they made, and then earnestly and fervently when he talked about the challenges for those who found themselves without a home.

The rest of the evening was spent on a series of little games. They took turns to pick songs and the rest of the table had to *Name That Tune*. Then they each told an embarrassing story, and the table voted on whose was the worst. Joy won, with a tale about the time she attended the opera and developed food-poisoning with explosive vomiting mid-row during a beautiful performance of an aria. April was crying with laughter by the time she finished the anecdote.

Pudding was meringue with fresh strawberries, and a cheese board complete with Paul's ginger and apple sauce. April ate both offerings.

They had been through three – maybe four – bottles of wine, as well as the Mai Tais, and April knew she shouldn't accept the glass of port offered to her but, in the end, she couldn't resist.

Chapter Fourteen:
Paul

Paul got out of bed at around ten, which was late for him but still a little early for his hangover. The shower helped, as did a large glass of fresh orange juice and two paracetamols. He was glad to have downed a pint of water when he came home.

He gave the place a cursory tidy, made his bed and opened the curtains and windows. Then he forced himself out of the house to walk to the newsagent and pick up a few groceries and a newspaper. It wasn't far, and the weather was ideally for it – warm, with a slight breeze, and patchily overcast. He still liked to read a physical broadsheet on the weekend, when he had the chance. Today would be perfect for it. Thank God they hadn't invited him over on a Saturday night: even the idea of cleaning while he felt like this nauseated him.

He got back from the shop at eleven-thirty, feeling much better and smiling to himself about some of the stories told the night before. It had been such a terrific evening he even contemplated inviting everyone to his for a return meal. He had never entertained in the flat before, and the thought of it was odd, unsettling, but strangely appealing. He was daydreaming about menu choices when there was a knock on the door. He knew it would be April before he even opened it. No one else ever came around unannounced.

"Oh my God," was the first thing she said. "I am so sorry." She was dressed in loose, striped pyjama bottoms and an oversized sweatshirt.

"Aren't you hot?" he answered.

"What?" She looked down at her top, its sleeves gripped in her palms by half-hidden fingers. "I wanted to feel like I was still in bed."

"Come and have some coffee," he said. "And tell me what you think you have to apologise for."

April sat on a high stool in the kitchen, cradling a coffee cup in her hands.

"I actually don't properly remember getting home. I remember saying goodbye to them, and I remember being in my bedroom. I was sat on the edge of the bed and for some reason I was debating whether to make myself a gin and tonic. Thank God I didn't. But anyway, I don't remember the bits in between. Or some of the bits before. I think I had a whisky after the port? Maybe two? I don't even know. How ridiculous. I'm thirty-bloody-two."

She closed her eyes and lifted one hand across her face, slopping some of her coffee onto her pyjamas in the process. She didn't seem to notice. He wiped up the small drip that fell onto the floor.

"You were fine," he said.

"Really?"

"Well, apart from wanting to go for a midnight walk and break into the park by jumping the wall. You were perfectly sensible."

Her mouth dropped open.

"I'm kidding!" he said. "You were no different from the rest of us at the table, and on the way home you hardly said a word. You just stumbled along prettily with a goofy smile on your face. Then I helped you unlock your door, and you went off to bed, I assume."

The word 'prettily' hung in the air between them, filling the brief silence.

"Anyway, I'm making pancakes," he said. "Want some?"

"Oh, man. I am such a failure. Rosie cooks up this phenomenal dinner and hosts it in her beautiful house — flat — whatever — and you're such a good grown-up you can knock up pancakes on a hangover." Paul was amused by the idea this was the pinnacle of adulthood, but also vaguely pleased with himself at the same time. "I don't even know how to make pancakes at the best of times. And I feel like absolute death because I don't know how to say no to mixing my drinks. How come everyone else has this adulting thing nailed, except me?"

He was already taking flour and sugar from the cupboard. "That's just the stale alcohol talking. Hasn't anyone told you that hangovers come hand-in-hand with imposter syndrome and existential dread once you're over the age of thirty?"

April stumbled off the stool. "Will you show me how?"

"Sorry? How to be an adult?"

"How to make pancakes," she said, sheepishly. Which did make rather more sense.

"Of course," he said. "I'm sure you'll be a natural."

They made the batter mix and she seemed surprised when he said, ideally, they needed to leave it for thirty minutes. She asked him what other insider secrets he had. He told her to make sure not to overbeat the mixture; how a flat griddle pan was best —

anything non-stick would work, but you needed to make sure there were no scratches on the bottom, or it would stick; make sure it was hot enough; oil was better than butter because butter burns easily. She listened carefully, seriously, standing close to him, and alternating her gaze between the pan and his face. It was charming.

While they waited for the last fifteen minutes, he made them Bloody Marys, reassuring her they were a one-off, and that she was still on holiday, so what did she care? They started to feel better after their coffees and large, cold glasses of tomato juice and vodka. He added both Worcester Sauce and smoked tabasco, and felt his mouth finally lose the aftertaste of too much white wine.

They ate three pancakes each with a second Bloody Mary and he was glad to see April finally starting to loosen up. She yawned and checked the time. He realised he didn't want her to go.

"I think I might be able to get back to sleep now and nap the rest of this off. Do you want a hand cleaning up?"

"No," he said, and he knew it was too quickly.

But she laughed: "OK, I understand. I don't think my standards would be quite the same as yours, either."

They stood, and he walked with her towards the door.

"Thank you for this morning. For the pancakes. And for being so... kind to me."

"You're welcome," Paul said. "Any time."

And as the door shut behind her, he had an image again of saying goodbye to her on her doorstep last night. How she had leaned forward and told him he

was a lovely man, and kissed him soft and long on the
lips before he pulled away.

Chapter Fifteen:
April

It was Monday. There were two weeks to go until the start of term, so April decided it was about time she popped into school to tidy her classroom and take down last year's displays. She hadn't yet made the journey from the new flat to work, and she needed to judge the best route and see how long it took. It was a shame Rosie no longer worked there, or they could have lift shared. It wasn't far, but it would take two bus journeys if she didn't drive, and the thought of doing that while armed with numeracy books was not at all appealing.

She went in around 9 am, having intended to set off at seven-thirty, as that was the time when she would be leaving home during term time. But her summer body clock simply did not comply. The journey took her twenty-five minutes – a surprisingly long time – and she vowed to try it at seven-thirty at least once before the start of the school year, to see if it was the same.

April arrived at a clean and quiet building and was glad at the lack of distraction. She started work with the radio on and the windows wide open. She sang along, loudly, badly, to some tunes on Radio 2. In the end, she stayed for the whole day, not realising the time, absorbed in putting new backing paper on the boards, fixing new labels to trays, getting a new stack of exercise books ready.

Her classroom was light but old. The school was well-maintained but not ideal for modern teaching, the space just a touch too small, with plug sockets in peculiar places. There was an old portable TV still on a bracket in the corner above her desk, and the entire floor space was filled with tables, as class sizes exceeded the ideal number. Everything was painted magnolia. She would have loved a proper, comfortable book corner and some modular furniture that she could slide into new seating plans as needed. And a mural. But she made do.

She had a new lavender reed diffuser that she placed high on a shelf behind her desk, out of reach. And she had bought herself some stationery: pens, a pencil case, a pot for her desk. All teachers love stationery, she thought, with a smile. She had chalk paint and she wrote a series of welcome messages on the windowpanes, hoping the cleaners would not be overzealous and remove it, as they once had. By the end of the day the room looked much better, and she was satisfied - and also hungry. Luckily, she had her own key, as the only other staff member on the premises – the Deputy Head – was long gone. At 5 pm, she reset the alarm on then building and locked up.

She drove home, irritated by the queues of traffic at each light and the constant test of her clutch control as she inched along. She vowed to make her return journey either earlier or later in future. Or perhaps she should reconsider her route. But by 6 pm she was home, and soon on her way out again to the local Chinese takeaway for noodles and spring rolls.

She came home at 6.30 and breathed a contented sigh as she flopped into her chair, happy that the day had been active and successful. She was about to tuck in, food piled high in an enormous dish she suspected was actually a serving bowl on her lap, when a text message pinged on her phone. She looked down to the screen absently, expecting it to be from Kelly. It was Tom:

Hi. Have you seen the email about the flat?

It was over a month since he had last texted and she had put the flat sale out of her mind, as much as possible. If he was texting, she assumed there was news. She knew she could not afford to put her head in the sand, she'd regret it later if she didn't look after her own interests, but really, she simply wanted it all to be over. To let him get on with it, and she would take whatever she was offered. She stared at the phone, the little black letters, formal and cold. No kiss. She moved her tray to one side — knew she wouldn't be able to relax until this conversation was resolved:

Sorry, I haven't checked my emails since last week. I've been busy with work and...

She paused, reflected, and edited the text to:

I haven't checked my email since last week.

She didn't need to apologise to him. He replied instantly:

Can you look at it, please?

Was that annoyance? Always hard to tell in a text.

I'm eating my dinner. Can't you send me the gist?

She watched the three little dots as he typed, and then saw his quick reply:

We want to reduce the price for a quicker sale. Suggest we drop by 40K. It's all in the email.

She had always said the price was too high. She was

the one who had been calling for it be lower, initially, but Tom had taken advice from a friend who dealt in property regularly, apparently, who told him it was a 'burgeoning area' and as it was in 'walk-in condition' (thanks to April) they should pitch it high. And now, somehow, it sounded as if they were trying to bargain her down. As if she'd need persuading. He was the one 'suggesting' a lower price. It was bizarre how things always seemed to be turned around that way. Now it sounded as if it was her fault it had been overpriced. Or was she being paranoid? Perhaps.

But the thing that truly bothered her wasn't any of that. It was the fact she wasn't sure who 'we' referred to. The estate agent? The lawyer? Or someone else.

April picked up her food again and turned the phone face down on the arm of the chair. She flicked on the television and called up a film on the planner. She had already decided what her reply would be:

Yes, go ahead. You know that's what I wanted in the first place.

But she wasn't sending it yet. He could wait.

*

It was still only eight-forty-five by the time the film ended. She hadn't replied to Tom, and she couldn't bring herself to do so. There was another message from him when she picked the phone up, but she vowed to leave it unread until morning. He was lucky to be getting off so lightly – she might just have easily called him back and bitten his head off. She decided to call Kelly instead. She carried her empty bowl into the kitchen and filled the kettle, finding her sister's number as it boiled.

"Hey, sis," she said.

"Hi! I was starting to wonder what had happened to you," Kelly answered.

"Really? It hasn't been that long, has it?"

"Considering we usually speak or text every day, yes, it has. I tried you on Friday night and you didn't answer. Then you didn't answer my text on Saturday, so I got the message and left you be. I know when I'm not wanted." She was pretending to sulk. "Out partying again, were you?"

Kelly was only teasing, but April knew she was genuinely curious. There was little about April's life that Kelly didn't know these days. A two-day silence would have filled her with questions.

"Yup. Actually, I was."

"Oh, really? I'm all ears. Just let me kiss this munchkin goodnight and you can fill me in."

April could hear Kelly's voice muffle as she seemed to cover the mouthpiece. Snippets such as: *love you too; I'll be in later; no TV; no; yes, that's fine; no one you know.* She came back on the line and sighed down the phone.

"Sorry about that. I couldn't tell her it was you, or she'd have wanted to commandeer you to tell you all about Jodie's birthday party. She had a real-life Princess there, don't you know?" Kelly made a little hurling sound. She was not a fan of Princesses.

"I think we should get a Queen for Olive's. Show them how it's done."

"I think we should have bloody Joan of Arc," Kelly said. "Anyway: tell me, tell me, tell me. Where have you been?"

April filled her in on the evening at Rosie's and the silly games and her monstrous hangover. She described the vibrant platters of food, the Mai Tais, Rosie's place. She told her how Paul had surprised her with his stories about his job and his lovely sense of humour. How he was better company than ever, now she had gotten to know him more.

"Glad it wasn't the gardener, then?"

"Absolutely. And the next morning he even cooked me pancakes, can you believe?"

Kelly spluttered, mouth full of some sort of drink. "You didn't stay over with him, did you?"

"What?" April laughed, shocked, "Absolutely not. Where did you get that idea?"

"Wind back then: how come he made you pancakes? Slow down. Give me everything. You know I live my social life vicariously through you. I'm glad to see you back in the saddle, it gives me something to pick over."

April explained how the evening had descended into port, and then whisky, and possibly something else. More wine? She wasn't sure. She had stuck to whisky, which she didn't even really like. She remembered picking at cheese and listening to everyone's stories, and how, at one stage, Rosie and Joy had been dancing in the living room while Paul and April sat at the table giggling, watching them through the open double doors, pretending to score their moves and critique them.

"I was pretty drunk. I think I was swaying a bit, and I know my chair rocked at one stage and I wobbled so he had his arm across the back of my chair. But he said I was no worse than anyone else, which is rather reassuring. I must go and see Rosie, to thank her, and see what she says. I had a fear she would be annoyed with me but Paul has assured me that's nonsense."

"I think this one sounds much more promising than the landlord. Not that there was ever a chance there, which is a shame. But then maybe not, if he's as grumpy as you say. Anyway, anyone who makes pancakes and coffee for your hangover is a keeper in my book."

"Don't be ridiculous. He's just a nice bloke." April was taken aback.

"A 'nice bloke' who puts his arm around your chair, helps you home, and then cooks you up breakfast in the morning. A 'nice bloke' who you spent half the weekend with. No, there's nothing going on there, at all…"

April didn't dare tell her about the Bloody Marys.

Chapter Sixteen:
Dai

Dai was determined to finish sorting everything out this week.

He had two more weeks off work and was due back in September. That seemed as good a time as any to go back, a bit like going back to school. But, also, it was as bad a time as any. He could not say he felt much better. Certainly not substantively. Would he always feel this way? He didn't know, but had to test the water, to see what would happen on his return. Some people said work helped them – a distraction. He hoped that would be the case for him.

When he was a child, his grandad had told him grief doesn't ever disappear, we just learn to grow around it. At the time he had no idea what he meant, of course, but Dai could still remember where he was standing when his grandad said it. They were in the dining room, waiting for his mum as she came in and out with various pots and dishes. She was ladening the table with more and more food. It must have been a special occasion, but he couldn't recall what. As a child, it had seemed like a banquet, a ludicrous amount of food – but perhaps his memory betrayed him. What he could clearly remember was the warmth rising up from those dishes, and the smells of overcooked vegetables, beef, gravy, heavy and overpowering, salting the air. He stood next to his grandad who sat still and upright, smiling and nodding each time his mum came into the room.

Then, while his mother made one last trip, his grandad had patted him on the head and said, "Grief doesn't ever disappear, son. We just learn to grow around it." And as she walked back in, he had reached forward to a dish of buttered carrots and started to mound them on his plate enthusiastically, telling his mother how wonderful it all looked, before turning to the next platter of food.

Now Dai knew. Now he knew exactly what his grandad meant. Grief becomes a part of us, it stays with us, inside, and we change. We accommodate it, and grow around it.

He steeled himself, then opened the door to her bedroom.

*

By the time Paul came at 7 pm as promised, Dai had actually bagged up four bin bags of rubbish to throw, and a fifth with clothes to recycle. It was painfully slow progress, but at least he had made a start. Perhaps he should have started in the bedroom in the first place, rather than the shed, where there were mostly sentimental items. The last few weeks, attempting to wade through the boxes out there, had been horrendous. Each time he had started, he failed badly, coming across mementos and memories. It had left him feeling bruised and burned for days afterward. This had been easier, in relative terms. But hindsight is a wonderful thing.

"Here I am, Boss," Paul said, as Dai opened the

door. He was wearing overalls and had a pair of rubber gloves in his hand. Dai stepped aside to let him in. Paul followed him to the bedroom.

"Rubbish," Dai said, gesturing to the four bags. "Charity," as he pointed to the fifth.

"OK, how about I put the charity in the boot of my car, and we leave the rubbish in the hallway outside? There's nothing... it's not... perishable, is it? It won't matter if it sits out there? We can take a trip to the dump on Saturday."

Dai almost raised a smile, listening to Paul's awkward attempts at being tactful. "Hey, it's been festering in this bedroom for weeks. Another three days is hardly going to make any difference."

"Right. And you'll have more by then, I'm sure," Paul added.

Dai was touched by this subtle encouragement. "I'm halfway through a suitcase. We could finish it together." The suitcases were the worst, somehow.

"I'm all yours," Paul answered, putting on his gloves, and breathing deeply.

*

An hour later, Dai was sitting at the table in the living room, eating an omelette Paul had just cooked up for him. Paul was walking around opening windows, shaking out rugs and throws. Dai left him to it, said nothing.

"I could get some groceries in for you next time I do a food shop. I don't mind," Paul said.

Dai paused, fork close to his mouth, and raised his eyebrows. "I appreciate that. But no need."

"I... listen, don't take offence, please, but maybe

there is a need. You've lost a lot of weight, haven't you? You'll be no good to anyone if you waste away." Paul was plumping the cushion on the armchair.

"Bit personal, mate," Dai said, in an attempt to lighten the mood.

Had he lost weight? He supposed so, but was surprised it was obvious. He only ever wore shorts or tracksuit bottoms these days. He wondered if his suits would still fit him. He hadn't lost that much, surely? He looked down, lifted his t-shirt slightly. A wrinkle of skin sat over a stomach that was concave, hard. It was a surprise. There used to be a pot belly there, a soft layer over the muscle.

"Well, the offer's there."

"And as I said, I appreciate it," Dai said. The thought of bags of shopping nauseated him, but sometimes you have to do the sensible thing. Perhaps he would take Paul up on his offer. But he couldn't think about that right now. Not today. He was spent.

"So, what are your plans, then? When do you think you'll get things straight?"

"Soon," Dai said. "By the end of next week." The thought of doing this for ten days hit him like a wall. One step at a time. One step only.

"You'll carry on again tomorrow, will you? Want me to come around again?"

Dai shrugged.

"I'll pop up. Just to check. You're back to work soon, aren't you?" Paul said, casually, as he started to pick up a few things from the table to put them away. He wandered towards the kitchen.

He seemed oblivious to Dai's rising irritation and disquiet. Couldn't he see he was exhausted? This was enough. He felt harangued. He wanted to be alone again. He wanted Paul to leave. "I told you. I'm going to carry on every day this week. Get as much done as possible before Saturday when we go to the dump. But it's not a quick job."

"Well, I'm impressed," said Paul, coming back from the kitchen with a tea towel in his hand. "Making a start must be the hardest bit."

Dai hoped so. He didn't think it could get much harder.

Chapter Seventeen:
April

Hey Rosie. Are you in for visitors early afternoon?

April was looking after Olive. She had been sick the night before last, and Kelly assured her that she had been fine by lunchtime the next day, but the nursery had a forty-eight-hour rule about coming back in when children had been off with a tummy bug. Kelly could not afford to take a day off when she had just returned from leave. So, it was Aunty April to the rescue.

She adored looking after her niece. This had been a cause of much confusion and teasing at first, as April had sworn off having her own children. Everyone in the family thought it was hilarious she went out of her way to offer to change nappies, wipe up spaghetti splodges, and take charge of the bedtime routine. Russ, Kelly's husband, kept making (mildly irritating) jokes about her biological clock and getting broody. Luckily, Tom had similar feelings to April and had no urge to father offspring. They simply laughed it off. But then, of course, she did love youngsters: that's why she was a teacher. She simply didn't want her own.

It seemed odd to her that people found it so hard to comprehend.

Today, she planned to walk Olive to the shop via

the park and pick up some food for lunch. Then, if she was lucky, Rosie would be in for them to pop round. All children adored Rosie, and this seemed like an easy solution to keeping Olive occupied. And she hadn't seen Rosie since the dinner party.

Her phone pinged.

Would love to see you but not back until after two-thirty – OK?

Great. I'll have my niece in tow. Hope that's OK? We'll bring biscuits.

*

They'd walked to the park, playing the car game. Olive won because she chose red, whereas April's purple had only yielded one car. Now Olive was rushing around, climbing as high as possible on every piece of equipment. The park was basic, but, of course, as Olive had never been here before she was suitably excited. She was straight in, and up, and down. After a while, she fell from the monkey bars and scraped her knee but, after a second of silence while she stared at the freckles of blood appearing, she seemingly decided crying would be less fun than continuing to play, so she jumped up and ran over to a sort of zip wire that stretched right across the playground. April was glad Kelly wasn't here to see this: she was, understandably, always a little nervous watching her daughter's escapades.

After twenty-five minutes of exploring, sliding, swinging, and stretching, Olive was grubby and panting. She came over to ask for a drink.

"Good plan, missus. Shall we go to the shop now?"

Olive considered this and seemed unsure.

"We could get ice-cream for after lunch." April held her palm up to Olive for a high-five, but she continued to frown. April pointed to her hand. "Hey! Party on the top floor. Give me five!"

Olive giggled and slapped her hand with undue force.

As they walked to the shop, Olive skipped alongside her and told her all the gossip from nursery. Joao was in love with Meelia (as Olive pronounced it) but she didn't love him back. Charlotte had a nut lalergy. They were going to get a new slide for the playground soon. A big one. April made a conscious effort to show interest and ask questions, reasoning that if she took her seriously now, perhaps her niece would continue to trust her as she grew.

At the shop, they grabbed rolls, cheese, and cucumber for sandwiches, and peanuts for a snack. "Don't tell Charlotte!" she whispered into Olive's ear, who nodded earnestly in response. April went to the freezer and was checking the ingredients of the various ice-cream tubs on display when Olive appeared beside her with a cake mix, drawn, no doubt, to the multicoloured unicorn on the front of the box.

"Oh, I think that's probably got lots of nasty ingredients in it, dude," she said. Paul's influence seemed to be rubbing off on her.

"Nasty?" Olive queried.

"Bad stuff. Sugar and chemicals."

"Does that one has chemcals?" Olive asked, pointing over to a box with a picture of a princess on it.

"Oh yes, and your mummy would kill me even if it didn't have chemcals."

Olive was frowning and looking at the packet

intently. "Mummy makes good cakes. We make cakes sometimes."

"I'm not as good at baking as your mummy is," April said, putting the box back onto the shelf. "I wouldn't know where to start."

"You start with butter. I can show you how." Olive picked up another box.

April laughed, instantly taking the box from her to put it back, and wondering if they would play this game with every packet on the shelf. She directed Olive away and smiled at the shopkeeper as they moved to the counter. Then she stopped. Why shouldn't she make cakes? How hard could it be? And they had some time to kill before they went to Rosie's.

"You know what, dude? Why not? Let's do it. What do we need?"

Olive grinned and jumped up and down, before taking her by the hand and walking her over to an intimidating shelf containing flour, sugar, and various little pots and bottles. With her help (and that of the shopkeeper, who reminded her to get icing sugar while scanning the products through) she ended up walking home laden with eggs and various cupcake ingredients.

*

First, they made the sandwiches together and then April put them in a tupperware box in the fridge.

"Sshh, little sandwiches. Have a nice sleep there and we'll come back to get you when we're ready."

Olive giggled. "Not eating them now, Aunty April?"

"No, Ollie. Remember I told you? If we make them up ready, we will be very pleased with ourselves when we are hungry later. And we can eat them while the cakes are cooling." She was also very pleased with herself that she had remembered you couldn't ice warm cakes.

"Night night, sandwiches," Olive said, patting the fridge gently. "We going to start with the cakes now?"

April took to the internet, typing in 'easy cupcake recipe' and clicking on the top link that came up. Between them, they laid out all the tools they would need in a line, in order of usage, leaving a gap for anything she didn't have. It was then she realised how poorly equipped her kitchen was for any sort of baking. There were an awful lot of gaps. She stood, staring at the counter, hands on hips. Olive mirrored her, forlornly taking in the sight.

"Right, dude. We can make do without a spatula, but I think a bowl and something to bake them in are pretty key to the process. But don't worry, I have a plan."

*

When Paul opened the door, he looked worried.

"Sorry, I know you aren't keen on unannounced guests. But we have a baking emergency on our hands, and I thought you were the man to help us."

Paul's face broke into a huge grin, and he dropped down onto his haunches. "Well, who's this?" He stuck one hand out. "I'm very pleased to meet you. My name is Paul, but my best friends call me Stinky."

Olive ducked behind April's legs slightly, but she was smiling.

April laughed, taken aback. "Hey, how come I have to call you Paul, then?"

He winked at Olive. "Come in. Tell me how I can help."

As they entered the flat, April realised it was the first time she had ever seen objects on the couch and coffee table. There was a laptop on a tray, some folders, a pencil case, and a phone.

"Oh!" she said, "You're working. Of course, it's Thursday. I'm lucky you're in."

He waved her away. "I'm fortunate in that I get to work at home sometimes. I have the benefit of both a minor lie-in and uninterrupted focus time."

April winced. "Whoops!"

"No, that wasn't a dig. It's about time I took a break. Don't worry."

They followed him into the kitchen, where he opened his white cupboards and produced everything they needed, without so much as a prompt from April, along with a few things she hadn't known she needed at all.

"Ingredients?" he asked.

"I think we're sorted. I'm only doing something basic. Vanilla, butter, sugar, flour. Even I should be able to cope with that."

"*Eggs*, Aunty April. We need eggs in cakes."

April blushed. "Yes, I do know that, honest. I have eggs."

He smiled softly.

"Would you like a hand?" he asked.

*

A little over an hour later, April was wiping down the surfaces of her kitchen. Paul was washing out the mixing bowl in the sink while Olive sat on the floor in front of the oven, willing the cakes to cook. The warm air of the kitchen smelt of vanilla.

Every now and then, Olive would turn to update Paul with a progress report. "They're getting bigger now, Paul," and "That one's got a crack in it."

Paul responded with appropriately dramatic noises, telling her to let him know when they started to go brown, and to make sure they didn't burn. April was mostly ignored, her little niece quickly ascertaining who the baking authority was, of the two adults.

"I didn't realise you liked kids," April said, watching the way he interacted with her niece.

Paul shrugged. "Why would you? And more to the point, why wouldn't I?" He turned to face her, amused. "Is this one of your 'I thought you were a boring old accountant' type assumptions?"

"Hey, I never said 'boring'".

"Or old?" he asked.

She made a little gesture with her hands: maybe, maybe not, it implied. He flicked soap bubbles at her.

"I don't know, I guess I thought the mess, maybe? The noise? That it would bother you. You don't strike me as the type to like chaos."

"Oh, I don't mind necessary mess. You can't expect to have kids around without a few splashes and accidents. And I can cope with other people's mess, as long as it's not too intrusive... I just choose to live my own life differently."

"So, it is a choice, then?" she asked, instantly regretting it.

He turned around fully. "What do you mean?"

"I wondered if you might have OCD or something."

"Or something?" he frowned, and looked down at

his hands.

"Sorry, I shouldn't have said that. I don't know what I was thinking."

"It's OK," he said, continuing to wash up.

"I thought, you know, rubber gloves and cleaning routines and bright white kitchens. They aren't the usual go-to style of men in their thirties."

"Right," he paused, looking at her. "You know, actually, I do," he said, turning back to the sink.

"You do?"

"Yes. I do have OCD. And there's no need to apologise. But I like to think it's not a disorder. At least, not for me, not at the moment. I have some coping strategies for when it starts to go in that direction, but it's been a long time since it's been out of control. It's a part of who I am now."

April stared at him, amazed at his candour. "That makes sense. You know, it was the nosiness I was apologising for. I'm not suggesting having OCD is shameful or something. It wasn't a 'sorry for suggesting you had OCD', it was a 'sorry for being nosy'... I sometimes say the wrong thing, so I am prone to apologies – don't know if you've noticed."

He laughed. She turned back to her wiping up, although most of the surfaces were sparkling now. She had one more question, and she couldn't resist asking.

In for a penny, in for a pound.

"So, you wouldn't change it, then? If you had the choice to get rid of it completely?"

"Do you know what?" he said. "I really don't think I would."

Chapter Eighteen:
April

Olive carried the box of cupcakes with great care, moving cautiously down the street, arms raised and proud. It took twice the expected time for April to reach Rosie's front door. April didn't mind, enjoying the sight of Olive's exaggerated footwork and the tip of her tongue poking through her pursed lips.

"Can we have one when we get there?" Olive asked, for the second time.

"Yes, Ollie. I'm sure we can." It had been a trying test of little Olive's patience to wait this long. She had done well.

Luckily, Rosie was well-versed in the secret language of children and understood exactly what she needed to do as soon as Olive passed her the box, saying, "We made cakes." They all marched directly to the kitchen and tucked straight into them, Olive's usual shyness around strangers overpowered by her desire for vanilla sponge.

"Well, this is a nice surprise. I was expecting shop-bought biscuits," Rosie said.

"We did go to the shop," Olive stated. "But we didn't get biscuits."

"I can see that! I didn't know your aunty was such a good cook."

"She's not," Olive said, picking butter-cream from

the top of her cake with her index finger. "But me and Paul is."

April laughed. "Very true, luckily for all of us."

Rosie raised her eyebrows. "Paul made these, did he?"

"Hey, don't you two go stealing my credit. I helped."

"She did the weigh-ying," Olive said, much to Rosie's amusement.

"I did need a lot of help," April said. "But I had some very good teachers."

Rosie finished making the tea, which had been intended to go with the cakes they had impatiently devoured. She poured Olive a glass of almond milk, which she viewed suspiciously but then sipped from.

"You two get on really well, don't you? Paul and you, I mean."

April considered this. "I suppose we do, actually. We don't know each other well. But it's nice to find someone who is easy to talk to. He is very... straight. You know where you stand with him."

"Absolutely. But he seems to have warmed to you quickly. It took me months to get more than a sentence out of him."

"Shame I don't have the same effect on the top floor."

"What's that?" Rosie was putting the teapot on the table, along with two handmade mugs.

"Did you make these?" April asked. Rosie nodded. "I mean Dai. On the top floor. He barely says 'hello' to me if he can get away with it."

"Oh, him. The dark-haired one, you mean. Shockingly handsome, isn't he? Shame. It's sad." She was shaking her head as she poured the tea.

"I've rather gone off moody men. I don't have much patience for them these days."

Rosie looked at Olive, who was dabbing her sticky finger into the milk while trying to use it, ineffectually, as some sort of spoon. "Shall we take this into the living room? Olive, I've got some DVDs in there that you might like, if that's alright with Aunty April?"

"Fine by me."

*

Olive was perched on a mound of cushions, which she periodically rearranged until she was boxed in the middle of them. Rosie had given her a choice of three films, and now bright colours and breezy cover versions of 60s songs were on the screen.

"I'm surprised she can keep her eyes open. I'm exhausted myself. This baking malarkey is hard work," April said. "Who knew?"

"April, you haven't told me what happened with you and your ex," Rosie replied.

"That's rather a change of tack!"

"Sorry, yes. I know. But what you said before, about moody men: I've been wanting to ask and, now the little one is occupied, I thought..." she shrugged.

Somehow, coming from Rosie, it was an inoffensive question.

"I did tell you," she said. "That day when we first bumped into each other, remember?"

"Ah, no. Not exactly. You told me you'd bought a flat together and it hadn't worked out. You said you drifted apart. And I was dying to ask... There's got to be more to it than that. I got a sense there was."

"It's not the most dramatic of stories," April

replied. "There's actually not much more to tell. Honestly."

"Listen," Rosie answered. "You are perfectly within your rights to tell me to keep my nose out. But I do remember how much you loved him, and I also know you aren't always the best at sharing your emotions. You always did bottle things up."

"Did I?" she asked, innocently. But she knew what Rosie was alluding to.

"Yes. I was there when you came straight back to work after your mum passed away. And I remember what happened later." Rosie's voice was low, and she was turned towards her, close. April couldn't bear to make eye contact with her. "I'm just saying, it's good to talk. And, despite appearances, I am a good listener."

"I know you are, Rosie... OK, I'll fill in the blanks. But prepare to be disappointed by the mundanity of it all."

As she told the story, and started to describe how hard she had worked on the flat, and how little time they spent together, and the way she had been decorating the place that Easter, it struck her it was hard to do so without sounding a little culpable herself. She had been completely absorbed in the flat renovation and hadn't paid him much attention. Perhaps she could have been more supportive when he first got promoted, it struck her. Maybe she was selfish in the way she approached everything.

Perhaps it wasn't entirely his fault.

That's no excuse for betrayal, of course. April would never think otherwise. But the cracks in their relationship went back further than that, and the rift would have existed, even if Susie hadn't been there to fill the void. It was possible to think his behaviour was inexcusable, and still accept some degree of responsibility for the break-up, she realised.

"I guess it's a small comfort that you weren't married with a child," Rosie said.

"In some ways. Initially, that just added to my feelings of failure – shame, even. I could not believe I was back to square one so quickly. No partner. Never married. No children. Rental property. I know it's ridiculous, but I felt embarrassed to be back where I had been in my early twenties."

Rosie nodded. "Not ridiculous. It shouldn't be embarrassing, but that is rather the way society makes us view things. In reality, those are hardly the hallmarks of success."

"Quite. Plenty of people have all those things and are no doubt far more miserable than we'll ever be."

"And others never have them at all. Which is fine too," Rosie said, wryly.

April nodded. "Besides, we never even intended to have children. We had talked about getting a bigger place at some point, and marriage, yes. But I have never been a 'big white dress' sort of girl so an actual wedding wasn't a priority. And the fact of the matter is that selling the flat is horrible enough. A divorce on top of it would have been a nightmare. That's obvious to me now."

"I've been there," Rosie said. "It really is. Divorce is horrendous."

"Have you?" April was shocked. "You've been married?"

She nodded, pointed to her chest. "And divorced."

"Wow," April said. "I had no idea. When?"

"I know. I don't look the type, right? I was married

118

very young – twenty-two – it only lasted three years. Unlike you, we did want children." She dropped her voice, glancing over at Olive, who was completely immersed in the film. "And they weren't forthcoming. Now that's a story for another time, maybe with a few glasses of red inside me." Her eyes were moist, and she flapped a hand in front of her face to will the tears away. "Anyway, enough about me. You know, I think it sounds a bit as if you fell out of love. And maybe you both changed. I have always thought you don't really find out who you are until your thirties."

"I hope you're right. I could do with a bit of stability. And happiness," April said.

"Oh, I'm sure it's just around the corner. Wouldn't you say you are starting to feel happy, these days? You seem good."

"Starting to, yes. I am battered. It's still a fresh bruise so little things can hurt. And annoyingly, I do miss him, sometimes. But I am definitely healing. I'm starting to think I could do with a second chance at love," she said. "I feel like I might actually get it right, this time."

"Ha! Well, we live and learn. You're probably right. And only hummingbirds mate for life."

"Do they?"

"Yes. Oh, but, and penguins. And swans. Oh, to be a bird…" Rosie waved her arm, expressively, her silver bracelets jangling on her wrist.

"It sounds *awful*," April said, with a smile.

*

Later that evening, April sat in her chair and picked at her third cupcake of the day, with a cup of herbal tea.

119

It had been a good afternoon spent with two lovely people. It was packed, and busy. And she was exhausted. So why did she feel so deflated? Tearful, even?

The house was still, and a slight breeze prickled the skin on her arms from the open sash window. Outside, she could hear the murmur of cars, and the occasional footsteps of people. But in Hummingbird House, and in her flat in particular, there seemed to be no noise at all. And – after such a bustling, cheerful day – perhaps that was the problem.

Chapter Nineteen:
Dai

It was Friday morning, and Dai sat at the little table in his living room, drinking a black instant coffee. He didn't like black coffee. He had no milk.

He knew he should be back in that bedroom by now. Every time he closed his eyes, it was all he could see. Her things. Her precious things, that he was throwing away.

Paul had come back the evening before as promised, and Dai had a feeling he'd be back again tonight. Possibly with shopping, as the look on his face when he opened the cupboard, optimistically looking for soup or beans to feed him – the eggs all being gone – suggested he was more than a little concerned. Maybe he'd bring some milk. Every cloud.

They had worked on two more suitcases. One of them, the case at the bottom, had crumbled and split in two when they tried to open it. For some reason, this had horrified Dai at the time, and he had started trying to fix it, furious tears on his cheeks. Angry with himself for breaking it; with life for taking her away. Paul had encircled his wrist with his hand to stop him – his long, gentle fingers made it much of the way around. Dai had stopped then, sat on his heels, and allowed Paul to reopen the case. He'd put on his gloves, and worked delicately, lifting the fabric inside

121

as if each piece was valuable, in spite of the stains and creases. And they were, in their own way. Dai had been truly touched by that simple act of kindness.

That's all they had managed to do: two suitcases. It took them over an hour, because the second case had been full of ornaments and other small objects, each wrapped in newspaper. Dai didn't want to risk throwing the lot. Some of the paper was twenty years old or more, crisp and yellow. He'd been tempted to keep it, but that would have undermined the purpose of what they were doing. He didn't let himself read the headlines. Didn't need any more distractions.

The idea of going back in there, that room, alone, made him feel sick. Maybe he'd go for a run. Clear his head.

But one more coffee first.

Paul had been telling him about that April girl. At first, he assumed he was wittering away to try to take his mind off things, but then Dai noted the look on his face as he talked, and how he stared off in the distance sometimes, picturing her, he guessed. It was sweet, really. He was almost giggling when he told some story about making fairy cakes, to which Dai was only half listening.

"Never really spoken to her," was all he could think to add on the subject.

"Oh, you'd like her," Paul said, enthusiastically. "She's sort of irreverent. Cheeky. But kind. A genuinely nice person, you know, when you get to know her."

"Right. Betty said similar. Glad to hear it."

And then Paul had returned to the newspaper and started telling him something about apple sauce, how he'd bring him some. Dai didn't have the heart to tell

122

him he'd be eating it out of the jar with a spoon if Paul ever did.

The second coffee actually added to his nausea. He got up and opened the curtains, realising with a jolt it must be mid-morning by now, and not early, as he had assumed. The sun was high, and it was a hot, clear day. There were cars driving by.

He hadn't even been out the building for a couple of days. Perhaps that was part of the problem. He was losing track – the battery in the living room clock had been dead for some time, the hands perpetually stuck in an angled, downward grimace. He had no idea where his phone was, and it would no doubt be flat.

He took his coffee and wandered into the kitchen to throw it down the sink before he had a chance to change his mind. Then he went into the little hallway of his flat and picked up the old trainers he left near the front door. He would go for that run. Now.

He grabbed his keys, zipped them into his jogging bottoms and went out onto the landing to do his warm-up routine. He always did his stretches out there, rather than on the street, as he felt there was a touch of exhibitionism in doing lunges and jumps on the pavement. He did a few jumping jacks and dynamic stretches, and then started a brisk walk down the stairs, building up to a small jog by the end of the first flight. He was about to sprint down the corridor to the next set of stairs when April stuck her head out of her flat door, forcing him to stop.

"Dai," she said. "I thought you were someone else, sorry. I… I'm expecting someone."

He was about to move off when she said, "But can I ask you a quick question?"

He did a little dance on the spot, as subtly as he

could. He was itching to go and didn't want to end up having to do more stretches out front. He nodded at her.

"Right, well, sorry. I... I'd like to paint some of the rooms in the flat. Is that OK? Nothing bananas. Just some grey. Maybe something brighter in the kitchen. I don't mind paying."

He wasn't sure how to respond. "Right," he said.

"So, it's OK, then? I'm allowed to do that? I thought I should ask you first," she asked, leaning towards him, quizzically. She was pulling the cuffs of her jumper into her palms. She must have been very hot, he thought. Then he stopped to look at her properly, and it struck him that perhaps she had been crying. Her cheeks were blotchy; her eyes pink.

"I'll get back to you," he said, and started to jog away. But he looked back briefly, and said, "April, take care of yourself."

"Oh," she said, behind him. "Thank you. You, too."

Chapter Twenty:
April

She knew it was something serious when he called instead of sending a text. Tom hadn't called her in almost two months. She let it ring for a long time, staring at the screen. She was tempted to ignore it completely.

"Yes?" she answered, eventually.

"Hi, April?" he asked, and the way he used her name, enunciated so formally and clearly, made her body flinch. She could hear him walking somewhere, perhaps out of someone's earshot. She said nothing. "Yeah, it's sold," he said.

"The flat?" she asked, needlessly, and kicked herself.

"The flat. I'm assuming you're happy with the asking price. We have a buyer. No chain. It's finally done."

It was finally done.

*

She had called Kelly immediately, who vowed to pop around at lunchtime. She said she could swing a long break as she hadn't had one at all, the day before. Besides, the boss was out for a business lunch and would be back to the office late, or possible not until the next day.

By the time she got there, April had her old jumper on and was eating another cupcake. She dragged herself down to the front door to let her in, still with cake in hand. Kelly launched herself at April and wrapped her in a huge hug.

"Come and tell me all about it," she said, and marched her up the stairs, holding her free hand.

Kelly made her tea and listened while she opined about how ridiculous it was to be upset. She really was nearly over him. She knew it sounded like she was over-protesting, but she truly believed it was true. And the flat sale was a good thing. It gave her options. It cut him out of her life altogether. So why the tears? It was frustrating.

"But that's the kicker, isn't it?" Kelly said. "It completely cuts your ties with him. It's the final step. No going back."

April teared up again, then picked up a cushion and smashed her face into it. "Ahh! I'm so annoyed with myself. I think it's because he seems so chilled about it. Like it really doesn't faze him at all. He seemed happy, if anything, by the end of the call."

"But don't forget, he had time to get used to it. This was out the blue for you. How long had he known?"

"I didn't ask," April conceded.

"It might have been bloody yesterday, or the day before, for all you know."

"True. I take your point," April said. "It was a bit of a shock for me. He was talking as if it would struggle to sell not long ago. That's why we changed the price."

Kelly nodded. "So, you weren't expecting it. And

126

it's not just him, is it? You absolutely loved that flat. You put your heart and soul into it. Think how much time you spent doing it up. It looked amazing. That's got to be a bitter pill to swallow in itself. Giving it up."

"Yup," April wiped away the remaining tears. "It feels like a big fat waste of time. And I won't even get to see it again. And I feel bloody stupid that I did it in the first place."

"It's not a waste of time. It's all experience – emotional and practical experience."

"What do you mean, 'practical experience'?" April asked.

"You can consider that your starter flat. The next one will be even better. You won't make any mistakes about how high you hang your pictures, or anything." April nodded at that memory. "And it won't have him it, being all moody and critical."

April tried to smile. "I think it's the future being gone that upsets me the most."

"Your future is not over. Not by a long shot," Kelly said, firmly.

"No, I know that. That's not what I mean. The future I was building for us – the specific future I pictured, thought we would have. That's gone. Those possibilities are gone. All those possible futures, they were just stupid dreams. And now I don't know what the future will be – I can't picture it at all. And… I'm sort of scare to, in case that turns out to be a ridiculous dream, too."

"It must feel scary. But you know," Kelly said. "That also sounds rather exciting."

*

At the end of Kelly's extended lunch break, April walked her down to the front door, grateful to have had her strength and chatter. She was in mid-flow about some beautiful flats being built near her house, and how April should go to see the plans before they were all snapped up. She meant well, but the thought of viewing property right now was overwhelming. As she stood in the doorway, hugging Kelly goodbye, she spotted Paul coming back from the direction of Rosie's with a small paper bag, no doubt full of apples or tomatoes.

She waved to Kelly as she drove away, and stayed in the doorway so Paul didn't have to fumble for a key. It was only as he approached, and she saw the look on his face, that she remembered she was in pyjamas with unbrushed hair, at lunchtime.

He was smiling, about to make a funny quip she guessed, when he saw her face. "Everything OK?" he said, genuinely concerned.

"Don't worry, my sister's calmed me down. I just had some… unexpected news. Not bad, exactly, but I wasn't really prepared for it."

She stepped back to let him pass and he dutifully came in. She shut the door and gestured to the stairs for him to walk ahead of her. She didn't want him looking at her PJs longer than necessary.

"Well… that's good, then. Good job," he said as he walked up the stairs. He sounded awkward, but she was touched by his concern.

"Still working from home?" she asked, for want of something else to say.

"Yes, finishing off a project, but I'm back in again from next week. I thought I should have a break from the screen. And I could feel the vegetables calling me."

"Paul, come to me… Come and squeeze my firm, fresh skin…" she joked, waving her arms. It was an attempt at a joke, but he blushed, and she wondered if she had overstepped the mark.

He was at his door. "Listen, if you fancy some company, you could come round here for supper tomorrow? I do have rather a lot of broad beans to get through for one person." He was looking at the bag, rather than her, and it seemed like the beans might be more of a concern than her mood. Nonetheless, she wasn't going to turn down a free meal from her personal chef.

"I'd love to," she said. "What time?"

Chapter Twenty-One:
April

It was Saturday, and April arrived at the out-of-town DIY store just after opening time, parking her little car close to the entrance. She was coming for tester pots and colour cards, hopeful Dai would approve her request to paint the flat. She was glad to be here before the throng, and pleased with herself for managing to act like a grown-up and get up early.

She was feeling more positive, having spent some time the previous night searching online for city breaks, and thinking how she could actually afford a week away in October half-term for once, now that the flat was sold. She couldn't even recall the last time she had been on a plane. Kelly had messaged her a few times, as had a good friend from work, and after a surprisingly good night's sleep, she had awoken feeling more positive. She was lucky to have sold the flat so quickly, and for a good price. She had a nice new home, healthy and lovely family, and thoughtful friends. She was determined to capitalise on this mood, and not let the 'existential dread' – as Paul called it – set in again.

She spent an age in the paint aisle and ended up with four different tester pots and a leaflet. She was about to leave when she thought, while she was here, perhaps she should get a few more bits for

Hummingbird House. The duvet beanbag was losing its novelty, and the sale of the flat and thoughts of buying somewhere new had made her realise she wouldn't be ready to move for several months yet. She needed to make the flat at Hummingbird House more of a home, as she had intended when she first moved in. She needed to invest in it, and herself. Besides, wherever she went, she was bound to need a second seat.

She grabbed a trolley. By the time she got to the till, the trolley was stacked high with cushions, two small folding side tables, a pot plant, a rug, several scented candles, a few other bits and pieces – and an actual beanbag.

*

That afternoon, she spent a couple of hours unpacking her new furnishings and the final two boxes of knick-knacks that had been stacked in her bedroom since she moved in. She had left them until last partly because they were full of fiddly little things that she wasn't sure where to place, and partly because she knew they would evoke emotions and memories. There were a couple of photos: Kelly and Olive, and another one of her mum on the beach, the warm glare of a 1970s shot showing her in a garish swimsuit. She was smiling at the camera; one hand shielding her eyes from the sun. Mum would have been younger than April was now, she realised. She placed the photo on the little table next to her chair.

She put a cluster of candles in the fireplace, as she had always intended to, and plumped two cushions on her chair. She took the fairy lights from her Bonnie

131

Bear tea party and placed them in a clear vase on her kitchen table. She looked around and admired her work. The rug took the edge off the hard floor. The beanbag by the fireplace looked cosy. It was starting to come together. April was trying to picture what type of artwork would best suit the space above the fireplace – thinking perhaps that she would even do her own – when there was a knock on the flat door.

Dai nodded but said nothing when she opened up. He was in his usual outfit of tracksuit bottoms and vest top, and he seemed to have been out running again. At least, that was suggested by the little spots of perspiration on his shoulders.

"Hi," she said.

"It's OK to paint the flat. Thought you'd want to know."

He lifted one hand to his forehead and swayed slightly. It crossed her mind that he could have been drinking, but she dismissed the idea. He didn't look drunk – he looked ill. The harsh light of the corridor emphasised the dark, deep semi-circles below his eyes, and his stubble had grown into an unkempt beard. He was pale. His hair fell down across his face, straggly and unwashed. He brushed it away, absentmindedly.

"Oh, great," she said. "That is good news."

"You don't need to pay. If you are happy to get the... get the..." he trailed off, then seemed to come back again. "If you're happy to get the paint, give me the receipts and I'll sort it for you."

"Really? That's very kind. I'm not trying to suggest the place is poorly maintained or anything. It's fine. But a new coat of paint would make a real difference, especially in the –"

It happened quickly, though perhaps she should

132

have anticipated it.

It was a heavy faint. Not a gentle swoon, with a bending of the knees, but a flat, hard drop, straight forwards. She tried to catch him as he plunged to the floor, managing to break his fall, at least. She held him briefly, his arms looped through hers, but the pressure was too much, and she couldn't sustain his weight. His body slipped from her grip and fell to the side of her, his face smacking the door handle as he went. Mechanically, she dipped to the floor and gently placed him into the recovery position. She was on automatic pilot, simply following what she had been taught as part of her job. It was a strange intimacy, moving his heavy, warm limbs into place. She expected him to rouse then, to ask her what on earth she was doing as she angled his arms and legs - but he stayed out cold.

Now what?

She jumped over him and went to Paul's door, but he didn't answer, even after some sustained banging, so he was clearly out. Unsure what else to do, she went downstairs to find Jonty and Ben. But as she reached the bottom of the stairs, she heard voices outside. The front door was open, and Jonty was chatting away to Betty.

"Hi – sorry – I need some help," she burst out, cutting through an anecdote about fishing, or eating fish, perhaps.

"Goodness, dear. What on earth's the matter?" Betty said.

"It's Dai," she said. "I think he's fainted."

"What! Where?" Jonty said.

"Outside my flat. He's still there —"

Jonty raced up the stairs, but April stood still for a

moment. Only now was the shock of what had occurred starting to set in. Perhaps it wasn't a faint. Had she even checked that he was breathing? What if she had done the wrong thing? She felt a tremor in her legs but refused to give in to it. She needed to stay in control.

By now, Betty was standing next to her. "Are you alright, April? Can I get you something?"

"No, thank you, Betty. I'm fine. I think I'd best go and see if I can be any help." She took a deep breath and went back up the stairs to see how Dai was now. Betty followed, gracefully and slowly, behind her.

By the time April reached her front door, Dai was propped up against the wall, awake but clearly groggy. Jonty was squatting down beside him, talking in a low voice, stroking his arm gently, almost tenderly. It was an odd sight.

"I'll get some water," April said, wanting to be useful, but as she started through the open door of her flat, she heard Dai say, "No, no."

"You want to get home, mate? Or do you think we should get you checked out?"

"Do we need an ambulance?" April asked.

Dai shook his head. "No! No ambulance. Give me a minute."

Everyone stayed in position, in silence. Jonty squatting next to Dai, Dai with his back against the wall, eyes closed, Betty holding the banister. They made an odd little tableau, and their calm demeanours belied the seriousness and stress of the situation.

After a couple of minutes, Dai moved as if to stand, pushing himself up with one hand.

"Careful. Let me help you." Jonty put one arm out for him to pull himself up with. April stopped herself from intervening, knowing manual handling advice would be poorly regarded at this moment.

Once standing, Dai stayed propped against the wall. But he was starting to look more awake.

"You sure you don't want water?" Jonty asked, gently.

Dai shook his head. "It's happened before," he said. "I'll be OK. Just need a bit of a lie down." He lifted his fingers and dabbed at his cheek, which had started to puff up around a small, sharp cut where he had crashed into the door handle.

"Let's get you upstairs, then."

April went ahead, ready to open his door, glancing back periodically to the peculiar sight of Dai, one arm wrapped around the shoulders of the older man, the other arm grabbing on to the banister with each step.

When she reached the top floor, she was surprised to find several full bin bags on the landing outside his flat.

"Paul will be back in a minute. He's helping me," Dai pointed at the bin bags and Jonty nodded, as if this made sense to him, though April was unsure what he meant.

She twisted the door handle and it opened, unlocked. She was disorientated briefly to find herself in a small corridor rather than going straight into the living room like in the other flats; but then she realised the lounge was in front of her, as hers was, so the bedrooms were no doubt to the left. She walked down the corridor, flicking the lights on as she went. It was dark and windowless, with a laminate wood floor. Sparce. She reached for the door handle of the first room and, just as she was about to turn the handle, Jonty, Dai, and even Betty, all cried out for her to

135

stop. She jumped.

Dai coughed. "Not that one. My room's next."

Whatever was in that first room, not one of the tenants of Hummingbird House was ready for April to see.

Chapter Twenty-Two:
Paul

Within moments of Paul's return from the first run to the dump, Jonty was standing next to him in the lobby, telling him about Dai's fall. He must have been sitting in his flat near the door, waiting to pounce on him. He was clearly shaken. Paul found it touching, but also alarming. The thought crossed his mind that he was glad not have seen this episode with Dai, but it was swiftly followed by a sensation of guilt. He should have been there for him.

"Fainted, he did. Refused to be looked over. Thinks he's just overdone it."

"Right," Paul said. "Has he eaten anything, do you know?"

"Not that I'm aware of. That lad is turning into skin and bone. He didn't even want water. He's clearly not taking care of himself. Did you know... he said it's happened before? And not that it's any of my business, but I should say he's stopped showering, too."

Paul nodded. "I know. I'll go and get him a shop in, and then pop up to see him. Hopefully he's asleep now. I don't want to disturb him straightaway." The rest of the bags could wait until the morning.

He walked to the local shop, glad of the excuse to be outside, and, in all honesty, glad to delay his visit.

137

He picked up soap, shower gel and a razor in the hope Dai might take the hint. He chose some easy foods: eggs, cereals, biscuits, bread, bananas, tuna, pasta. Perhaps he might be able to persuade him to cook up a big pot of something that could keep him going for a few days, though he doubted it. Dai had always been a stubborn old so and so.

Paul went up to the flat as soon as he got home, not stopping at his own. He tapped on the door, gently. He didn't expect a response and was about to try the handle – Dai usually left it unlocked – when he appeared in the doorway, in a dressing gown. A fresh, blue bruise was appearing on his right cheekbone.

"Hello, I heard about your little trip and thought I'd bring you some sustenance."

Dai grunted. "I hope you got some milk."

*

Two hours later, Paul was sorting Dai's washing. His bedroom was smaller than Paul's, and more cluttered. There wasn't room for the bed to stand freely in the room, so it was squashed against a wall. Paul pulled it out slightly and yanked the covers down, to air them, and thought they probably needed changing.

It seemed Dai had given up on putting things in the drawer or wardrobe. There were a few odd items jammed in poorly shut drawers, socks hanging down dejectedly. The wardrobe doors were open, showing that most of the hangers were empty. Clean clothes were on the chair; dirty clothes on the floor. At least, that appeared to be the system. Paul placed a fresh pair of trousers, pants, and a t-shirt on the bed, next to deodorant and the new razor. He closed the drawers and doors, opened the window, and tidied up. Then he carried a bundle of clothes into the kitchen, to place them in the washing machine. But there was no powder, of course. One more thing to pick up for Dai tomorrow.

Paul had persuaded him to have a shower by finally coming straight out and telling him that he smelt bad. Dai had actually laughed, then lifted his arm and taken a sniff of his armpit. He seemed shocked to find Paul was right. "OK, mate. I shall rectify that straightaway."

Paul had stood, readying himself to leave, when Dai said suddenly, "Do you... do you think you could stay while I use the shower? Just in case?"

"I think that's a very sensible idea."

So now he was pottering around, waiting for Dai to emerge from the bathroom, and half expecting to hear the sound of someone collapsing.

Dai was in the shower for at least twenty minutes. For a little while, Paul stood at the door, listening, wondering if he had tumbled again. When Dai came out, he had one towel around his waist and another across his shoulders. His skin was pink. Steam poured like dry ice from the bathroom into the corridor.

"Better?" Paul asked.

Dai nodded. "You're a good friend. You can go off duty now. Don't want to take up your whole Saturday."

"Oh my God, Saturday! April's coming round."

"You'd best go get yourself spruced up then, mate," Dai said, with a half-hearted smirk.

Chapter Twenty-Three:
Paul

It was hard to switch off from the events of the day. Paul had a sinking feeling, knowing Dai was upstairs alone, and how much there still was to do before he was due to return to work. He had suspected for a while that Dai was going to need professional help of some sort – what exactly, he wasn't sure. But he seemed to be making painfully slow headway with everything. Perhaps someone to pack up her belongings? Or some sort of emotional support? Maybe the doctor? Probably all of the above. The trouble was he couldn't imagine Dai conceding to any of it.

Ironically, he had driven to the dump feeling more positive than he had in a while. He had a boot full of bags and two old suitcases, plus a broken portable TV. Dai had even cracked a smile at Paul's poor joke about the back of the television being so large you could empty it out and wear the whole thing as an astronaut's helmet. Dai had relinquished it easily, which Paul took to be progress.

On the journey, which was a good twenty minutes each way, his mind had drifted through all sorts of random, unconnected issues. It was good to switch off, he realised. Good to be out and about. He felt useful. Hopeful.

Perhaps this wasn't only a breakthrough for Dai, but for him, too.

The last few weeks he'd been more sociable than he had in years. Since Jennifer. But it didn't scare him, and he was proud of that. It had been easier than he had expected.

When he'd been with Jennifer, he had been at the height of his culinary career, working as a Head Chef. He worked long hours and irregular shifts, but they used to go out for dinner once a week at least, even though they could never plan exactly when. They had vowed to do this, to spend quality time together, and he felt she deserved it, somehow. He knew she would have liked to spend more time with him, and it was his work that got in the way – antisocial as it was. Their pact also forced him to be more spontaneous, and she teased him about it. It would usually be mid-week, sometimes even a Monday – a day bound to reduce the number of restaurants that were even open.

They took it in turns to choose where they went and kept it secret from one another until they were in the car. This very car, that Paul still had. The person who picked got to be the non-driver. Much as he hated to admit it, he remembered that weekly routine with fondness. She would tease him about going to a greasy spoon or the worst-rated restaurant in the area, and he would regularly threaten to take them to a Michelin-starred eatery that would cost a week's wages.

One time he actually did that. On her birthday. It did not go well.

He shuddered.

But that period of his life was quite a long time ago, now. In all honesty, sometimes he even struggled to picture her face. He hadn't bumped into her for two years, maybe longer, and he thought perhaps she had moved away. And he didn't mind. He was over her and the broken heart he had inflicted on both of them at the time. He was over the relationship, but it had left him with habits that had developed into entrenched ways. And it seemed easier to stay that way than risk the torture of heartbreak again. Than to risk hurting someone the way he knew he had hurt her. It had been a bleak, brutal time in his life.

By the time he arrived at the dump, he was considering how far his life had moved on in a short time, lately. For years, the social side of his life, such as it was, had been the same. Which is to say, almost non-existent. He went to occasional work dos, and visited a friend for a boozy weekend once or twice a year, but most of the time he drank a bottle of wine and watched a film on a Friday night, at home, alone. And he sometimes went for long walks alone on the weekend, though not as often as he would care to admit. He had been content that way. Happy? Maybe not. But he had not been bothered by it. He had simply plodded along.

Yet now, amazingly, he was socialising with all sorts of people. Nice people. There was Rosie and Joy. He had popped round with tomato chutney a few days after the dinner party and they had invited him in for coffee. He had accepted. And it was good.

He'd even gone for lunch with one of his colleagues this week. His idea. And it was fine.

At the dump, he pulled over as indicated by a man in fluorescent overalls, and jumped out of the car to get the bags from the boot. In spite of the smell, the grime, he couldn't help but grin.

Because then there was April, coming round again today. Which would be lovely. Wonderful, even.

He didn't imagine he was going to start branching out, embracing music festivals or weekly trips to the pub, for example. And he knew he would always want – no, need – periods of peace and quiet in nothing but his own company. But perhaps there was a middle ground, after all.

So this was the proof he needed, foolish man that he was, that spending time with other people did not always lead to stress, or arguments, or heartache. Not always. Not necessarily.

Which meant the possibilities were endless.

*

He had made a broad bean salad with feta and mint, and was about to put a simple gratin in the oven, when April arrived. She was early. He hadn't even changed.

She held aloft a bottle of prosecco in one hand and a box of chocolates in the other when he opened the door. She had her hair clipped up, with loose strands around her face, and her cheeks were flushed pink.

"Don't tell me off. I know I'm not meant to be here for another twenty minutes, but I feel a bit peculiar after Dai's escapades today, and hoped you wouldn't mind me sitting in the kitchen while you cook. Please."

"Come on in," he said. "It must have been quite a shock."

"Thanks. I'll be quiet as a mouse." She closed the door behind her and followed him back to the kitchen, already breaking her promise by pumping him with questions. "He's OK now, isn't he? I'm guessing

143

you've called in on him?"

"He's… as well as can be expected. Oh, and he's showered. Those are his towels in my machine." He gave a wry smile and lifted one foot to gesture at the washing machine. He had worn gloves when he put those on to wash.

"Showered! That's good." She smiled, knowingly.

He took some glasses from the cupboard and pointed at the prosecco. "Now?" he asked. "Or is it too early?" He hoped she wouldn't want to wait.

April sat on a stool. "Not too early. It's been calling to me all afternoon." She was watching him closely as he peeled the foil away. "Paul… can I ask you something?"

He felt himself stiffen briefly, wondering what was coming next. She had a habit of being direct. "Sure," he said, hoping it sounded casual.

"Is he ill?"

He put the bottle down briefly, then picked it up and started to pour their drinks. "What do you… why do you ask that?"

"I was thinking about it. Every time I see him, he looks a bit thinner. And he's always sweating. And you guys… you all… well frankly, everyone treats him really kindly, considering how… how he is." She held her hands up, and looked him in the eye. "Sorry, but he is rather… brusque."

"Yes, but there are reasons for that," he said.

"Obviously I don't like seeing anyone in that state. He was a right mess today. I wouldn't wish that on… Anyway, so I was wondering, what with the faint and all, is he sick?"

"Not in the way you mean, no," Paul answered, taking a sip of the wine.

144

"Ah," she said. "I see."

"You probably don't see everything. You couldn't because you don't have the full picture. But it's not my place to tell. It's personal. Though you do get the gist, I'm sure. He's... not himself. And he's not been looking after himself. We've all seen the change in him, and we are sorry to see it."

"Right," April said, frowning slightly.

"He wasn't always 'brusque', as you put it." She was about to interject but he brushed it away. She was right: coming in this summer as she had, Dai must have seemed a gruff, brutish creature. Paul knew different. "Don't worry. I understand. Just give him a chance, and he might surprise you. Hopefully. I really hope he will get back to his old self."

"OK," April said. "You told me something similar once before. I think I should trust you. I mean, I think I can trust your taste."

They clinked their glasses together.

*

He hadn't bothered to change at all in the end, and he didn't mind. They ate as early and quickly as they could, the pair of them wolfing down ciabatta and salad, gratin, and butternut squash, and knocking back the prosecco. It was what they needed.

Just an hour later, they were about to open their second bottle of the night. April was chatting away about her previous flat and how she had ended up in Hummingbird House. She was opening up, but he felt comfortable with her and glad that she seemed to trust him. Paul stood to collect the bottle opener from the drawer and, as he glanced out of the window, he saw

145

Dai carrying a bin bag in the garden. Paul was unsure what to do. He didn't want to worry April, or irritate Dai by interfering, but he had hoped – no, assumed – that he was resting, or eating. Not prowling about. His heart sank.

Paul watched as Dai went into the shed with the bag, and then swiftly came out again, still holding it. He sat on the ground, tore open the bag and started rummaging.

Paul said nothing and opened the wine, but every ten minutes or so he found an excuse to glance out of the window to check what Dai was up to. He found it hard not to be concerned, all things considered.

Chapter Twenty-Four:
April

For some reason, she had launched into the story of the flat sale in infinite detail. How she had made the place her own, how she had never expected it to sell so quickly, the reality of now looking to buy on her own. At first, he seemed absorbed and interested, leaning forward with concern, nodding at appropriate moments, not speaking much. But, after a while, she noticed his eyes had glazed. And he seemed fidgety. He was getting up often, packing things away, looking outside, distracted. Perhaps she should have spared him the details. Was she boring? Over-sharing?

"I'm sorry, I'll shut up about it now. It's hardly the most exciting tale of woe."

He sat down and touched her arm. "No, no. Not at all. Sorry, I've just... got something on my mind. Carry on." He seemed sincere.

"The truth is, plenty of people rent in their thirties, right? And not all of them have a generous deposit-sized hunk of cash coming their way. So, in that respect, I shouldn't complain."

"Quite," he said, widening his eyes briefly. She realised she had been tactless once more.

"Sorry. Foot in mouth again. You've never wanted to buy? Or... or had the opportunity?" she asked.

"When I changed profession, I took a sizeable pay

cut. So, it wasn't really an option. But, thankfully, I live a reasonably frugal existence. In the last couple of years, now I'm in this role, I have been saving up a bit. So, I probably could buy, but I'm in no rush. I like it here. And…" he trailed off.

"There are some upsides to living like a monk, then?" she teased.

"I'm not sure monks drink Sancerre."

"So, what is it about —?" she began, but then the sound of raised voices cut through the air and Paul jumped up. He raced to the kitchen window.

"Damn it," he said.

April got up to join him, following his gaze down into the garden. There was Dai, standing next to a heap of junk and wood, with a can of lager in his hand. He was agitated and seemed to be speaking to someone just out of their view. Or perhaps he was shouting to himself – it was hard to tell.

"Is he drunk?" April asked.

Paul scowled briefly. "He's upset," he corrected.

"Yes, of course. Sorry." She looked up at Paul, "Should we go to him?"

Paul didn't answer. He walked over to the kitchen door and flicked the light switch off. "Sorry, I'm not being weird. I just don't want him to know we're watching. He'll be mortified tomorrow."

She nodded. He came back beside her, and the pair of them huddled close at the window, standing in unison in the warm night, suddenly in cahoots together. She felt her chest tighten, and her breath reduced to little bird breaths, afraid to make the slightest sound, and thrilled by the sudden intimacy of the situation. She felt a touch of shame to be excited at Dai's crisis, but it was true.

Paul leaned forward and gently pushed the window further open. Dai's voice travelled up to them.

"Yes, I bloody can. She's not here to stop me, is she? She's. NOT. HERE." He threw something small down onto the top of the pile he had made.

There was a second voice, April realised. A low, calm sound. She inched forward to listen in but could not make out what it was saying.

"No. I've made up my mind. This has to stop," Dai yelled, bringing both hands to his face, and then bawling, almost roaring, an indistinct sound beyond words. It rose to a crescendo and then he was crying, shoulders jolting up and down as the sobs took over his body. Paul brought his hand to his own mouth and shook his head.

The second voice was there again, slightly louder this time, and April realised it was a woman. She looked directly down beneath the window to see Betty moving along the slabs of the garden path, coming into full view as she edged towards Dai. Betty. Of course.

"Look, David, that's true. But maybe not tonight. Leave it as it is, and sleep on it. You can decide in the morning. You've had a difficult day and…" The rest of her speech was lost in the night as she lowered her voice again.

She was in a dressing gown and slippers, moving cautiously towards him as one might a wild animal, but he moved away from her and stalked off into the shed.

"I don't understand –" April began, but then Dai appeared again with a canister of petrol, or diesel perhaps, and started to tip it onto the mound he had made. His intention became painfully clear. Betty stopped in her tracks. And they all watched in silence,

149

the hidden pair upstairs in Paul's kitchen, and Betty, helpless, in the garden, as Dai struggled to light a match – trying three or four times before it sparked – and then dropped it onto the bonfire.

The fire caught in a swell of flames, wider than she had imagined it would be. It was instant, huge, bright, and Dai stood for a moment – a little too close – before he moved back towards the shed again.

"Stay here," Paul said, with one hand on her back. "Please. I'll try not to be too long." And then he was gone, racing off into the night to try to calm their landlord who, drunk, confused, sick as he was, was burning someone else's possessions in the garden at nine o'clock at night.

She picked up her drink and watched.

Chapter Twenty-Five: Dai

He wasn't going to wait another week to get to the bloody dump. He was sick of this stuff everywhere, the mess, the memories. He wanted it gone. He had tried to sleep all afternoon, but he could sense her things around him, throbbing through the wall in the next room, glittering and gleaming in the garden shed. He had to get it gone. A fire was the best way to do that; it was so obvious now. The quickest, and the most final. It would be messy, noisy, fierce. It seemed fitting.

Betty had stopped trying to talk him out of it. At least, he thought she had. Perhaps she was still talking. All he could hear was the splutter and spitting of the objects on his pyre. It was reassuringly large, and plumes of black smoke clouded above it. So perhaps she was still talking, but it was too late. Nothing would stop him now that he had begun.

He went back into the shed and stood for a moment, taking it all in, determining what to burn next. His punch bag stood to one side, with a small circle of clear floor around it. But the rest of the space was a mound of bags and boxed, cobwebbed and fusty. He grabbed another bin bag, randomly. This one appeared to be full of fabric — probably the contents of that suitcase they'd emptied the other day.

It was over-full and starting to split.

As he came back out of the shed, something caught on the door, whether the bag itself or an errant piece of fabric, he wasn't sure. He didn't stop to look. Either way, the bag ripped further, tumbling curtains and tablecloths onto the floor. He had no time for this, and gathered it all back together in his arms. He noted then that one piece had caught on the handle. He yanked it, but it didn't come loose. It began to rip. He yanked again.

"Mate. Steady on." It was Paul. How long had he been there?

"Leave me be," he said, giving one more tug. The fabric stayed put, hooked, so he left it as it was and marched over to the fire, creating a stream of fabric from the door to the pile as he marched back.

"Dai, listen, we can come back to this in the morning," Paul was saying.

He dropped the entire bag onto the fire, wondering briefly if it would quash it, overwhelm it, but was then satisfied to see the already torn bag burst and ripple as it was consumed by the flames. Then the fire took hold of the worn fabric.

"Whoa!" Paul was shouting. He grabbed Dai by the arm and yanked him away, roughly. Dai staggered backwards, and only then did he realise the cloth was still caught on the door handle, and was stretched taut as a tight rope all the way from the fire to the shed.

"Shit," Paul said, looking around, futilely. "We need to trample on it or something. Betty!" He ran towards her, away from Dai. "Have you got some towels?" His voice drifted away, and Dai stood, mesmerised, watching the fire as it danced along the fabric rope and then took hold of the shed door.

*

Everyone was there: Jonty, Ben, Betty, Paul, and April. They stood in the garden, spread out and quiet, like broken chess pieces in an unfinished game.

The fire was out.

The fire service had arrived quickly, within minutes. April had called them, he heard. Someone had said so. He couldn't remember who. He should thank her. She had seen it all from Paul's kitchen window. Of course, they were supposed to be having dinner together, that was right. He should apologise for ruining their evening. But now the police were taking statements from people. They were being kind, and it seemed almost perfunctory, the way they were questioning. Systematic.

When they first arrived, and saw the petrol canister, there was a brief moment when Dai thought he might be arrested. The two officers had glanced at each other pointedly, and their first questions were fixated on whose possessions were in the shed. Was any of it valuable? Was it insured? Had he done this on purpose? No, it wasn't his stuff. And yes, he had, he said, he had wanted it all burnt. But then Paul had explained he didn't mean while it was still in the shed. He was taking things from the shed to the fire and hadn't meant it to burn down.

They went off with Paul, away from Dai, talking earnestly. He could see the male officer look over to him every now and then. He wondered what Paul was saying – though he could hazard a pretty good guess.

The police gave him a ticking off for being reckless and said they may well be back with more questions

153

the next day, but it seemed they were satisfied there were to be no arson or malicious damage charges.

Technically, they were his belongings now, since Mum had died.

Chapter Twenty-Six:
April

It was almost two hours from the time the fire had taken hold of the shed to when the emergency services left. The first hour flew by, a confused and nebulous haze of questions and activity. The second hour dragged, as she kept thinking, hoping, that it was over, that they could go inside and stop looking at the shed, the burnt skeletal contents of boxes and bags, and the sight of Dai pacing and crying.

The fire crew had wanted to be sure the flames were completely extinguished, they explained, as no one could be entirely confident of what was in some of the boxes and bags that hadn't been destroyed. They needed to ensure everything was safe, that the fire wouldn't take hold again, and nothing would explode.

The shed was now a pile of ash, rags, broken crockery, and fragments of photos and paper, all encased in sodden, charred timber.

Paul had a minor burn on his hand where he had grabbed a lump of wood that had shot out of the fire into the grass with a crack. He had instinctively picked it up and thrown it back to try to stop the fire spreading further. He had refused treatment and said he didn't want to go to hospital. He had been in receipt of worse burns in the kitchen, he said, and he knew how to look after it himself. She suspected it was worse than he said.

Jonty and Ben had been the first to go. They had only arrived on the scene as the services appeared, so had little to add to the details. They hugged Dai, and patted Paul on the shoulders, and then shuffled off home, a little worried that Oxo would be stressed by the events of the night.

Betty was next. She had made everyone Earl Grey or chamomile tea, depending on their orders, and then excused herself for bed. Before she left, April saw her and Dai locked together in a hug, him crying again, her talking softly into his ear, stretching up as far as she could to comfort him.

Finally, Dai shook hands with the firefighters and thanked them for their time, and then, with head down like a guilty dog, he allowed April and Paul to lead him back home.

*

It was a slow journey back to Dai's flat, as they had to go out and around the terrace so as not to traipse through Betty's place. And Dai was walking sluggishly, almost staggering: whether the effects of shock, beer, or light-headedness, she wasn't sure. They walked along in silence, Paul absentmindedly cradling his right hand in his left, and April clutching her arms around herself now that the temperature had finally dropped. Or perhaps it was something else that made her shiver.

When they entered the building, she had a sudden fear of being alone. It seemed too abrupt an ending for this dramatic night.

On the first landing, near Paul's flat, she turned to

them both. "Do you want to come in for a night cap or a hot drink?"

"That's not a bad idea. I don't think I'll be getting much sleep tonight," Paul said.

"Count me out," Dai said. "Sorry." And he started to walk again, ambling along past April's door towards the staircase. He wobbled briefly and stopped to clutch the banister.

"Whoa! How about we see you home, eh?" Paul said, rushing up to him and putting one arm around him. April followed. It was the second time today Dai had been helped up those stairs.

On the top floor of Hummingbird House, the stack of bin bags had grown and was in disarray. Some gaped open, their contents spewing out onto the floor. Now there were old suitcases in the corridor, too, along with some aged and broken cardboard boxes. Dai's flat door was open: it must have been so for the whole evening. She squeezed past the two men to turn on the lights in the flat, and watched them as they entered.

Paul let go of Dai, the narrow corridor making it impossible to walk with his arm around him anymore. Dai kept himself straight with one hand on the wall, supporting himself as he went. Paul followed behind.

April listened as Paul started to chatter away to his friend, teasing him about not messing up his bedroom as he'd only just tidied it for him, and saying how he'd ruined all his hygiene efforts from earlier in the day as he was now honking of bonfire smoke. She guessed he was trying to distract him. They approached the door she had almost opened earlier that day, the room that no one had wanted her to see.

It was open.

Paul and Dai walked by it and carried on to the end of the corridor to Dai's bedroom.

But April stood in the doorway of the other room, mesmerised. It was crowded, cramped, stacked floor to ceiling with carrier bags, suitcases, bin bags and boxes. She could see old magazines, records, plastic gadgets, tinned food. There was a laundry bag half-filled with old cutlery. A bird cage used to store socks and tights. The small patches of floor that were visible had balls of dust, fluff and hair entangled together in heaps.

Only one small space was clear, on the right side of a double bed; the left was covered in plastic bags. There was a dirty sheet, a single pillow without a case, and a blanket thrown back as if someone had recently got out of bed and simply walked away.

Chapter Twenty-Seven:
Paul

April had seen the room, so she deserved an explanation, Paul reasoned. That, plus the events of the evening, must have left her with no end of questions. It was amazing it had all been kept from her this long, in truth. He followed her into her flat, wondering where on earth he could start. It was the first time he had been inside since the day he invited her and her sister over for coffee. It looked different.

"Make yourself comfortable," she gestured at the chair. "I'll take the beanbag. I'll be back in a sec."

He sat down, wondering if it would be rude to ask for antiseptic or a dressing, as she seemed to have forgotten his hand, but when she came back, she was carrying a washing up bowl filled with water and a hand towel.

"I think maybe you should soak that for a minute because it's been left untreated for so long. It's dirty, isn't it? Mind you, it'll sting," she said. She placed the bowl on a small table beside the chair and waited for him to place his hand in it. On reflex, he yanked it back out as soon as it hit the lukewarm water. She chuckled. "Come on, soldier. Just for a minute and then we can hold the towel on as a compress. But I want to see it clean first."

She remained standing next to him as he put it back

159

in. Once she seemed happy that he wouldn't be taking it out again, she pottered off into the kitchen. He could hear the clink of glasses and bottles, and the rustle of a packet.

When she returned, she had a bottle of whisky, two glasses, and a large bowl of crisps.

"Just what the doctor ordered," he said, examining his hand through the dirty water. There a large white blister in the centre of his palm.

"I'm going to change that water. It's filthy already," she said. "Then I'll pour some whisky and you are going to explain to me what the hell just happened with our landlord."

She took the bowl away and came back with a fresh batch, this one cooler. She dipped the towel in to form a compress of sorts.

"Why do you always call him that?" Paul asked, as he took the towel and pressed it onto his hand. He felt himself grimace again.

"What?"

"Dai. Why do you always call him 'the landlord'? I thought it was some sort of street nickname I didn't understand at first. But... do you actually think he *is* the landlord?"

Her eyes widened. "Street name. Ha!" she said, amused. "Get you. But... Well, isn't he?"

"No," he said, bemused. "He's just a tenant, like you or me."

"Are you... are you sure? He showed me around the place and gave me the key. I just... why did he do that? And why did he offer to sort out money if I painted the flat?"

Paul smiled. "Do people always have a reason to do things? I promise you he is definitely not the

160

landlord."

April slumped back and sipped her whisky. "Wow, the dude must think I'm really weird. Some of the things I've said to him." She put one hand across her face.

Paul laughed. "He won't mind. He did it because he's nice. I kept telling you, he's a nice bloke."

"Right. You do keep saying that. So, he's just a tenant then."

"Just a tenant. Oh, and my cousin."

*

They sat in April's flat for hours, finishing the bottle of whisky while he talked, and then considering moving on to rum but, thankfully, thinking better of it.

Paul told April how Dai had lived here first, moving in with Doreen, his mum, when her health had deteriorated. Later, Paul had moved in to help out and support his cousin, when his flat had come available, too. It seemed sensible, and they had always been close. Their families spent most weekends together when they were growing up, and there was one summer when Dai had even lived with them in his teenage years. There was just eighteen months difference in age, between them.

At first it worked well. He popped in on Doreen whenever Dai had lots of work on, and he sometimes brought the pair of them food. They ate together on Sundays each week.

"Work? What does he do, then? I've never seen him go to work," April said.

"He's been off work since Aunty Doreen died. He's an accountant." He couldn't help but smile at the memory of April thinking this was *his* profession. Dai was always the white-collar worker, not him.

"So, she was a hoarder, I take it? Is that the right term?"

Paul nodded. "She used to live in a flat on the outside of town, but she was evicted."

"That's awful," April said, shaking her head.

He considered this. At first, he had been furious to hear what was happening, and had ranted about the Equality Act and mental health, and all of that was still true. But he also pictured that landlord. Remembered him well.

"Yes, it is awful. There is little help with this sort of condition. And a lack of understanding, for sure. But this particular landlord had been pretty supportive. I wouldn't want to paint him as the Devil. He was kind to her. Then she started leaving things in the corridors and the lobby of the flats. It was… spreading.

"One day, another tenant couldn't get her buggy in. and she complained to the landlord. When he came, he found the bathroom in Doreen's flat was unusable, the bath full of rubbish, the sink was being used to store old cans of food. And she was blocking fire exits, that sort of thing. He gave her a final warning. He offered to refer her to agencies. He even offered to pay for a deep clean once she'd sorted herself out. But he came back a month later and, by all accounts, it was worse." April was staring into her glass. "He said he found rat droppings."

"Wow," she said. "Ouch."

Paul pictured him vividly. The look on his face when the place was empty again, the carpet stained in places and fresh in others, where it had been buried under Doreen's objects. The wallpaper was damaged by damp, where mounds of clothes had been piled against the wall for months on end with no ventilation, the windows blocked, dirty. The landlord had simply stood there, mouth open, shaking his head. Paul offered to pay for it all to be redecorated. He had thought for a moment the landlord might cry, whether from the state of the flat, or Aunty Doreen, Paul still wasn't sure.

"It's a mental health disorder, I know. But why? What triggers it? Or... is it just one of those things?" April asked.

"It's an illness, yes. She... she had always been a sort of... procrastinator, I guess. And then she became more absent-minded. I remember when she was young, she would verbalise her actions as she moved. Thinking aloud. 'Now, I'll just go over here and put the kettle on... oh wait a minute, I shall do this first...' that sort of thing. And it was always a bit chaotic, what she said. She kept changing her mind, even when speaking it out loud. I thought it was funny when I was little. I thought it was alarming by the time I was a teenager."

"So, it came on gradually, did it?"

Paul wasn't sure whether to disclose all the details, and hesitated. But he had come this far. "Her own mother – my grandmother – she died very suddenly and young. Looking back, I think that was a big part of it."

"Oh my... oh, how awful," April said.

"Doreen found her," he finished.

She gasped. "Christ."

He nodded. "She was close to her. It's not like her mum died and it turned her into a hoarder, but I think the shock of it, the tragedy, it was something she

163

didn't get over, ever. And initially she had all her mother's belongings. She had stacks of them in her living room, in boxes and suitcases. And she wouldn't let anyone move them, or sort through them."

"Suitcases," April said, vaguely.

"Yes."

They sat still for a moment.

"So she came here to live with Dai – or they both came here – and then you moved in. And she passed away recently? Is that right?"

Paul nodded.

"Why do you think he's reacted so badly?"

"He blames himself," he stated, simply.

"But why? What happened?"

"It was cancer. Ovarian cancer. She'd probably been sick for a while because it was advanced when it was first diagnosed. She'd lost weight, and he finally persuaded her to go to the doctor when her belly became distended. Huge. I think Dai had told himself it was some sort of acid or stomach issue. No doubt they were both in denial about it. Anyway, they operated, but they couldn't remove all of the tumour as it wasn't contained, and then..." His voice broke.

April moved the beanbag closer to him and rested her head on his thigh, patting his leg.

"Look," she said. "I know I'm a nosy bugger, but you really don't have to tell me all of this. I get the picture now."

He shook his head fiercely and continued. "There's one more thing you don't know. Let me... I think it's good for me to... So, she came home, and they were considering treatment options. She was saying she didn't want anything. The operation had really floored her, and she was in her late seventies by then. There was nothing they could do to cure her, but it would have extended her time with us."

"Would have...?" April said, still resting her head on his leg. He touched her hair with his left hand and let it fall through his fingers.

"Yes. But she wouldn't even let him go into her room by then. She buried herself away. Dai was getting frustrated with her. But I still think he thought she would come around and accept the treatment, eventually. He thought she just needed a break, some space. By that stage, she spent a lot of time in her room. They rowed about it. His patience was thin."

"Not the best place for a sick patient, I should think," she muttered. "I can understand his frustration."

"Exactly. It was filthy. By the end, it was as bad as it had been in her previous flat, really. We had cleared so much out when she first moved, and we tried to come up with all sorts of strategies and tips to stop it all from recurring, but it didn't help. Nothing we did seemed to help. Leading up to the operation - or at least, in a few months before it, before she got too bad - she was out and about every day, coming home with bargains and trinkets. So, in her sick bed, she was lying in the midst of... Well, you've seen it."

"That's awful," April muttered.

He took a deep breath and ploughed on. "It turns out, she had an infection. In the wound. A huge infection. Rife. And she must have known, but she didn't tell anyone. Dai went to work one day, and when he came back, she was gone."

"Oh my God. How hideous." April's eyes filled.

"Bacteria in the room, no doubt. And it probably would have been cured by some bloody antibiotics."

165

"You don't know that, though. Not really. She was old and fragile. It sort of sounds as if she'd had enough. She gave up."

"Yes," he said. "I think she did."

She looked up at him from her seat on the floor. "Poor Dai," she said. "And poor you, too."

Chapter Twenty-Eight:
April

She slept until after midday, but still woke with a
pounding head. She could smell the smoke ingrained
in her skin and permeating her hair; and on top of
that, the stale, sweet taste of whisky filled her mouth.
She lay still for some time – half an hour at least –
trying to piece together and process the extraordinary
events of the last twenty-four hours. This was real,
violent, and concrete. It made her bickering with Tom,
and his not-quite-an-affair, seem flimsy in comparison.

After a while, she made herself a strong coffee
which she took back to bed, and then she sent her
sister a text.

Kelly didn't respond with a message: she called
straight back.

"Bloody hell, April," was the first thing she said. "A
fire?"

"Yup. It's certainly not the sleepy little house I
thought it would be when I first moved in," April
answered, croaky-voiced, as she propped herself up
with a pillow.

"But you're OK?"

"Of course I am. No one was hurt – except Paul,
but it was one minor burn. It was the garden and the
shed that took the damage."

"Unbelievable. It was a real fire, then? A proper

blaze? I don't think I've ever seen an uncontrolled fire," Kelly said.

"It certainly was. I'm sure it could have spread if we hadn't called the fire brigade. Actually, it was me who made the 999 call. That was a bit surreal. But everyone was really helpful, and they got here literally within minutes."

"Is he unstable, then? Or vindictive?" Kelly asked.

"What?" April asked. "Who?"

"Dai, I mean."

"Possibly the first, but definitely not the latter. It's a long story. Paul and I stayed up for hours afterwards talking about it. It seems… there's a lot that led up to it. Difficult circumstances. He has been through a lot."

"You sound a bit more sympathetic than I expected."

"I am. I'll happily admit I was wrong. You were right. Paul was right. He's not a nasty bugger after all. He's just… hurting."

"I can't believe it. How close was it to the house? So, listen, I've got a sproglet wanting her lunch here, but I want to hear all about it – and I want to check you really are OK. I know what you're like. Are you free this evening? I could come round. We can get a take-away. It's about time I was off duty."

"Yes, that sounds lovely," April said, already planning a long, hot shower and several more coffees that would fill the afternoon until then.

*

They went straight to the kitchen when Kelly arrived. While the view of the garden was not as direct as from Paul's, the wreckage from the previous night was clear to see. The scorched ground showed how close the bonfire had been to the shed, and the speckled patches of black on the grass suggested it could have spread further if they hadn't intervened. They stood next to each other in silence for a moment.

"Christ," Kelly said, clearly shocked.

"I know. It looks like a capsized boat, more than a shed, doesn't it?"

"You're right! That's exactly what it looks like."

"I should say we all had a lucky escape."

The wood was blackened and tarred but the entire space was still sodden; water sat in puddles dotted around the garden. The few cardboard boxes that were left in the far corner of where the shed once was were crumpled and collapsed in on themselves. Everything that had been closest to the shed door was completely destroyed and beyond recognition.

They plated up the food and took it into the living room to eat on their laps. Kelly listened, agog, so enthralled by April's story that she let her noodles go cold. April explained about Dai being Paul's cousin, and Doreen's carer, how she had struggled, and he had tried to help, but failed. How he blamed himself that he couldn't cure her or help her. How he blamed himself that she got an infection.

"That's a pretty major burden to bear," Kelly said. "I can't imagine. Hardly his fault, though. You can't cure someone who is that ill, not just by force of will. And doesn't it seem sad how little help they had? It's like they were left to try to solve it on their own." Kelly shook her head.

"They had Paul," April corrected.

"Oh, yes, your lovely Paul." April pulled a face to her. "I meant professional help, or Social Services.

Mental help. Visitors. Support. The woman was clearly unwell, and the family were struggling, but they were expected to manage."

"I can imagine there's not a lot of sympathy out there for hoarding. It's the butt of a lot of jokes, isn't it? And those television programmes where the people are presented as something to be gawked at, like a freak show."

"Like a freak show at best," Kelly said. "Dirty or lazy, at worst."

"Yes. Not that I can claim to be an expert, myself."

"So the one and only bit of good news," Kelly said. "Is that your landlord is a nice bloke, after all. He really is Mr Darcy: misunderstood and a little depressed." She flopped backwards, dramatically. "I'm so relieved. It would have been a waste of a handsome face if he'd been a nasty sod."

April laughed. "I think he might be more like Mr Rochester. Oh... and it turns out, he's not my landlord."

"What? Jeez, this place! Any more secrets or scandals you'd like to fill me in on?"

"Not really. Except I know you only have eyes for Dai, but I've finally admitted to myself I've got a major crush on Paul. But I think you've guessed that already."

"Two steps ahead of you there, Sis. I think the only person who didn't know that was you. Even Olive said she thought he was your new best friend."

Now April just needed to figure out if he felt the same way.

*

After Kelly left, it was still only nine o'clock, though April was exhausted and achy from the previous night's events. She was surprised not to have heard from anyone in the building; the sudden intense familiarity of their shared experience made it seem odd not to have been spending time with them again. She was tempted to go to knock on people's doors, but then restrained herself. Perhaps everyone was holed up, shampooing their hair furiously and reflecting on what had occurred.

The afternoon had been a dozy one for her but, at the same time, she felt like she had become clearer than ever about where she stood and what she wanted to do.

She was about to enter the last week of the school holidays and knew she needed to use her time wisely. There was still a lot to do regarding the flat and prepping for the start of term. But she wanted to enjoy these last few days before she was thrown back into the spin cycle of school life.

She grabbed herself a notepad and started to make a list. There were a couple of big-ticket items she needed to tackle, and it was time to make a plan.

Chapter Twenty-Nine:
Paul

It was late, about eleven, and yet Paul couldn't sleep. His body was both wired and exhausted. He was uncomfortable. His legs were restless, a crawling sensation under his skin making him kick out periodically to try to shift it. This was useless. He finally gave in and got up. He ripped the covers from his bed, convinced he could still smell, smoke saturated into the fabric, and took them into the kitchen.

He stood still in the dark, watching the kettle boil for a cup of tea. He couldn't bring himself to look out to the garden again. He had spent an hour this morning, poking through the debris to find anything salvageable. The ground was sopping and uneven. It was a sobering experience. At one stage, Ben had come out and half-heartedly joined him, but neither of them knew where to start, or what to say. Paul was almost relieved when he found there was not much to reclaim. The fire had done its job, at least. And it gave him an excuse to stop.

Dai was calm when he spoke to him after that. Resolved. This, at least, was something. They sat together and drank black coffee, and he was amazed by his demeanour. He was not the overwrought, tender man from bedtime, or the angry, floundering beast from earlier that same night. He was steady. He was even showered, without prompting. He was thin, pale, delicate. But there was something of his old self back there, inside

Paul was tired of looking after him, he realised. He was tired of being the stable one. It was his job – he knew that – and he had no right to complain. Dai was his only cousin and, really, they only had each other. He would do the same for him in a heartbeat. And, certainly, Dai was the one who had been through the biggest trauma. But that didn't change the fact Paul was simply exhausted.

After he had seen Dai, he came back home and showered again, and had intended to call on April, hoping she was not shaken up too much and also that he hadn't overwhelmed her with his messy family history. But he had nodded off on the sofa, which was unlike him but perhaps unsurprising. He hadn't woken until the evening and, by the time he had eaten his first food of the day, it seemed too late to show up.

He wondered what she had been up to. He wondered how she was feeling today. He swung between imagining she would be delighted to see him and the spark of quiet confidence between them would still be there today - and wondering if she could have woken up thinking him an oddball, a fool.

He thought back to Jennifer, remembering the mistakes he'd made there. So many. So obvious, now. He had been unsure with her, even from the beginning. He had allowed himself to go along with it, it was flattering, and easy, and he had loved her, yes. But not in the way she had loved him. Not with the open, ardent, joyous way she had. He had always known that. So he had spent his time since wondering if he really did deserve another chance. He got it so very wrong before. He had hurt her so much, perhaps it was only right that he stayed alone.

But he wanted to see April. He wanted to speak to her. Because in spite of all his openness and honesty last night, he still had a few things to get off his chest.

Chapter Thirty:
April

It was Wednesday, and she was sitting outside Hummingbird House with Betty, drinking elderflower cordial in the late afternoon sunshine. They had been there for at least thirty minutes already, drifting from comfortable silence, to random little facts that popped into their heads, to plans for the following week. It was a disjointed, comfortable, easy conversation. There was no pretence. They had not once mentioned the fire.

"I'm back at work next week," April said. "So, I'll have to pop into my classroom tomorrow and start to get my head back into everything."

"Do you?" Betty sounded surprised. "That seems rather a shame when it's your holiday."

April shrugged. "It's better that way. I'll regret it if I don't. The first week is always intense. I dread to think what it would be like if I was unprepared."

"Tell me, what sort of things do you need to do?"

"Clear my emails, finish sorting the first week's lessons, photocopying, getting resources ready, tidying, get to know the profile of my class. Better to be forearmed."

Betty seemed interested. "Do you like your job?"

"Yes, I do," April said. "But I'm vaguely thinking of moving on, to a new school or a new challenge.

The time seems right." It was the first occasion she had voiced this aloud to anyone, and as she did so, she realised how excited she was by the thought of it.

"Why not?" Betty said. "You must do these things while you are still young. But being a teacher sounds like awfully hard work these days."

"Yup. But then, lots of jobs are." April lapsed into silence for a moment. "Do you know, I thought Paul was some sort of number cruncher or Civil Servant when I first met him. I never would have imagined him as a chef or helping to run a charity."

"Really?" Betty asked. "You do surprise me. I wonder why?"

"First impressions, I guess. He struck me as a bit serious when I first met him. And sort of... bland. Anyway, it seems my judgement isn't always as secure as I once thought. Me and my sister also had a bet that Dai was a carpenter or craftsman of some sort."

Betty chuckled softly. "No, he's not the best at taking care of wood, now is he?"

*

They sat quietly for another ten minutes. April enjoyed the warmth of the sun on her skin and listening to Betty to her about the flowers in the pots on the patio. After a while, Jonty arrived home.

"Enjoying your last few days of freedom, are you?" He called as he came up the short path. April had seen him just the day before and told him how she was working up to the start of term.

"You've got it in one," she answered. "I won't be sunbathing at four-thirty this time next week."

"Betty, we should have one of our barbecues for

176

April this weekend. Might give us all an incentive to do a bit of... tidying up. Sort things out." He pointed to the rear of the property and gave a stage whisper, "You know, *out there*."

"Do you have plans, April?" Betty turned to her.

"No, not me. Sounds lovely."

"Well, then. I think you could be right, Jonty. We should give the summer holidays a bit of a send-off."

"Great," Jonty said. "I love a good get-together. Maybe we can persuade Dai to join us. Have either of you seen him since... since Saturday night?"

"Yes, I have, actually," April said. "I popped up to see him and ended up staying quite a while. He seemed OK. As good as can be expected anyway, or better perhaps. We ended up having a long talk."

"Good," Jonty said. "He's not been the chattiest in the last few weeks now, has he?"

"I feel like I've finally started to get to know him," April said. "He's a nice bloke. I think I might be able to persuade him to join us."

"Oh, you don't need to tell us, April. We know what a nice young man he is," Betty said.

"I know. Sorry. Obviously, you all know him much better than I do... I'm also sorry I didn't listen to everyone earlier."

April had been up to see him on a whim, having heard him padding around his flat for a while. It made her feel uneasy, wondering what he was up to and how he felt, picturing the room, boxes stacked and closing in. She could hear a little pitter-patter, like mice in the attic, and it drove her crazy imagining miserable scenes and dark endings.

She had wondered if he would even open the door to her, but he did, and he asked her in.

His living room was sparsely furnished, though not as bare as Paul's, of course. He had a small table, creating a dining area at one end, and a huge sofa. There was one floral, high-backed armchair. She didn't sit in it, wondering if it could have been Doreen's. The space was neat but gloomy, with curtains half-closed and windows shut. The air was stale, almost gritty.

He offered her coffee, and joked that she should take him up on it as it was the first time in months that he'd had ground coffee and milk in the place. He was calm, quiet, not exactly friendly, but not as brusque as she had known him to be; or perhaps she was looking at him through fresh eyes now. It was hard to tell. Maybe he had always been this way, and it was she who had the wrong impression all along.

Once he'd brought the coffee into the living room, he turned directly to Saturday night. He was apologetic, earnestly checking again that she wasn't injured or upset. He described it as "lancing a boil", and said he felt a little better now that there had been a crescendo, an "eruption". She had nodded. It made sense, in a way.

She asked about his mum. At first, he flinched when she mentioned her. He withdrew, seemed reluctant to discuss her, and April thought perhaps she had lost him again, that his new amiableness might disappear. But then, when he realised she was asking what Doreen was like, what she enjoyed, what she looked like, he opened up. She saw him smiling for the first time ever, genuinely grinning as he talked about his mum.

"I'd love to see a photograph of her," she had said. And it was true.

He got up immediately to collect one from his

bedroom. It was framed; a simple family picture of him with his parents, standing outside a funfair or amusement park of some sort. He was grinning, in short pants and chubby of knee, proudly holding a large stick of candy floss. His father had one hand on Dai's shoulder, and his mum was looking down at him, smiling affectionately.

"Is your dad passed, too?" she asked, wondering as she did so if he would consider this prying.

He glanced down to the picture and rubbed his father's face with his thumb. "My dad died almost ten years ago, now. I had a lot longer to get used to it, though, as he was poorly for a long time. And somehow, it wasn't the same. It sounds awful, selfish, really, but the fact she was my last parent, my only surviving parent, made this even worse. Does that make me a horrible person?" He looked up at her.

"Not at all. I know exactly what you mean. My parents are both gone. My mum died about four years ago, and I miss her every day. And yes, there's something dreadfully lonely about finding yourself orphaned at a relatively young age. There's this feeling that… that somehow there are no adults left to look after you. You look around for a grown-up to help sort things out, and realise the only grown-up is you."

He smiled. "Yes. And that is very — what's the word? — exposing. It makes you vulnerable. I always feel like I'm playing at adulthood. I don't think I will ever be the proper man my father was. I will never be a true adult, sensible and all-knowing, like my mum. I feel like a child in fancy dress, half the time."

"But I think we all feel like that, don't we? So I hear, anyway. It's imposter syndrome. You never know: perhaps they felt the same way about *their* parents."

"And their parents about the generation before? Maybe." He sighed. "Thanks for coming round, April. And letting me talk. Thanks for… for not diminishing her into the mad lady in the attic. She was more than that."

"Of course she was. So, what's next for you, now?"

"I think I'm going to get a skip. And most of it can go. I'll pay someone to help. And then, I don't know what... I might even move. And I'm due back at work next week. I don't know if I'm ready, but I think I'm as ready as I'll ever be, so I'll only be delaying the inevitable if I push it further. I have to go at some stage. It'll only get harder if I don't go back soon," he said, pushing his hair back from his eyes.

"Do you know what, Dai? I think I've had a really clever idea."

Chapter Thirty-One:
Dai

There was a rap on the door.

"Ready?" April asked, grinning broadly at him.

"Umm… yup, I guess so."

He reached down to pick up his trainers from the hallway, and as he did so he spotted her sandals: silver, pretty. He saw his shoes, dusty and grey, and was struck by how tatty they looked. They'd been dropped together, one resting comfortably slightly atop the other, the frayed ends of the laces frazzled, muddy and tangled; one shoe missing its innards. And when had the soles started to come away like that?

He held onto the door frame as he slipped them on, laces still tied.

"Do you think we could go to a shoe shop after? I need to invest in some new trainers."

"Thank God you said that," April replied. "I was dying to say something. You may as well be tying bits of old canvas onto your feet."

He laughed. "Any other little titbits of sartorial advice you'd care to share with me?"

"Oh, don't worry," she answered, as she turned away. "You won't be wearing those tracksuit bottoms for much longer, either."

They went down the stairs together, and he had to hold the banister - this time not from light-headedness, but because he was consciously fighting against the urge to jog. It seemed odd to be walking for once, but he was glad to be in no real rush, strolling out comfortably with April by his side. He needed to practice these things, if he was going to get back to the 'real world'.

She was asking him how he was feeling about going back to work, when Paul's door opened in front of them.

Paul jumped slightly when he saw them. He kept one foot in the door: an escape route, perhaps.

"What are you two up to?" he asked.

"Don't you ever do any work?" April teased in reply.

"Actually, I work very hard, thank you very much. I'm tempted to make a joke about teachers and holidays but I'm not sure it's safe to risk it."

She pretended to give Paul a punch to the arm, which landed in the air close to him.

"Got that project done yet, mate?" Dai asked. He knew Paul had been struggling to balance things recently; he realised how much he had added to his cousin's stress. Hopefully, not for too much longer.

"Onto something else equally fiddly, sadly," Paul answered. He turned to April. "Going anywhere nice?"

"Wouldn't you like to know? Nosy," she replied, then turned to Dai and winked, "Come on, mister. We'll be late." She pulled his sleeve to guide him away.

As they walked down the last flight of stairs, April started jogging ahead in what Dai took to be a mockery of him. He looked back to his cousin, hoping to share in the joke, but instead saw an expression on Paul's face he had not seen in a very long time.

Dai was finished before her, which wasn't surprising, but he didn't mind the wait.

It was the most lavish haircut he had ever had, coupled with a professional shave, something he had never bothered with before. But now he thought he might be hooked. It had been indulgent and relaxing. He had a traditional hot towel shave, a shampoo, and a much overdue haircut. He declined the manicure, with a chuckle. The young woman who washed his hair did so tenderly and unhurriedly and pushed down onto his scalp with her tiny fingertips to massage his head. It was almost embarrassing. But after a moment to adjust, he had let himself fall into it; just as he did with the steaming towel and the way his face was shaved shiny and clean by a hairy, tattooed man who had to stand within kissing distance to do so.

He managed to persuade the barber to keep a little length on top, but it was still a shock to see himself afterwards, the sides cropped down and fading from skin to speckled black. He looked fresh. And he looked thin. Younger, too.

April was having her hair blow-dried when he came over, and he assumed that meant she was almost finished, but then the hairdresser took some small clippers and started to razor-cut her neckline and even the ends of her hair. She had lost a great deal of length. The hairdresser picked up the flat black hair straighteners and gave it all a final once over.

April laughed a little when she saw him. Not cruelly, but happily, a little tinkle of laughter she tried to suppress with her hands to her mouth. "You look

183

amazing," she said. "I hardly recognise you."

"I take it that's a good thing," he said, admiring himself in her mirror, and striking a pose.

He sat down nearby and picked up a magazine from the table. This was the busiest place he had entered in weeks. Maybe months. It was disorientating. The music was too loud, the lights too bright, the people too hip. He was still lightheaded a lot of the time, and moving around this space – alien and harsh as it was - was like walking on a ship. But she was right to have suggested it. He couldn't spend the rest of his life in Hummingbird House. This was a good transition back to work, in a way, where he would be in an office full of staff, filled with radios, laughter and the gentle ping of emails.

The hairdresser finally held up a mirror behind April and then spun her chair around, brushing her neck and removing her robe. She looked even more like her sister than usual, he realised.

"You look amazing," he said.

"It's my back-to-school hairdo," she said. "It won't last." She put a finger to her lips and looked at the stylist, who was still fiddling with the back of her hair.

"Mine either."

"Right then," she smiled. "We've got an important trip to make." She stood up and slipped one arm through his as they marched towards the till.

Chapter Thirty-Two:
April

It was Saturday, the day of the barbecue. April spent the morning in bed, knowing she would soon have few opportunities to do so, with school fast approaching. Even Saturdays were busy during term time. She thought how glorious it was to have no one here to see her, and judge her, and make her feel guilty about her decision. Perhaps she could get used to this, after all.

When she eventually got up, the call of coffee drew her to the kitchen where she also grabbed a slightly stale pain-au-chocolat. As the kettle boiled, she admired her handiwork. She had been chipping away at the paintwork in the kitchen over the afternoons and evenings of the last week and it was almost done. The room looked larger, and more hygienic, though neither was true.

It looked like a clean slate.

She seized her new tray, and took her coffee back into the bedroom, where she snuggled down into her duvet, encased in a cover she had bought on a whim during her trip out with Dai the day before. It still had creases from the packaging – no doubt Paul would have disapproved –but she loved the crisp feel of the cotton. She flipped her pillow to the cool side.

It had been a success, she thought. They had

enjoyed one another's company and ended up spending even longer than they had expected together. They had chatted about light things: the last holiday they had taken – she could, hardly recall hers - their favourite restaurants, the best crime programmes. He talked about books – he liked John Le Carré and Graham Greene – and she was surprised, and rather pleased, to see him light up as he did so. It was the first time he had ever reminded her of Paul, it struck her. Their passion. Their sudden, pure, uncharacteristic openness when they felt something fervently. That ardour, that honesty. It was intensely attractive. Something she hoped to see more of.

*

She finally got out of bed just before midday and went straight to the shower. The bathroom remained untouched, but she was used to it, with the noisy fan and stiff silver taps. She put a shower cap on, to try to save her blow-dried hair and get an extra day from the hairstylist's work.

She was unsure what to wear to this barbecue, as she had been told by Dai that they were all expected to pitch in with loading the boot of Jonty's Jeep with the remnants of the shed. Jonty and Ben had taken charge of the whole mission, and she was glad of their kindness. Being on the periphery of events that night, perhaps it was easier for them to do so than for the others. Certainly, for Paul and Dai.

Betty was making a strawberry shortcake as a reward, she had heard. She was pretty sure that Jonty would have had something to do with that.

They were all due to meet at around two-thirty, the

boys estimating that an hour's work from the five of them should do it. She thought that highly ambitious, but hoped they were right. Then they would be firing up the barbecue and – as legend would have it – likely to stay out in the garden until ten or eleven at night.

She felt a little ridiculous admitting it to herself, but she was excited, and wanted to look her best, and so she wondered how she could dress up without making it too obvious. How she could be appropriately dressed for clearing debris, and yet somehow catch his eye. April took her time picking her outfit, laughing at her own schoolgirl behaviour, and wondering if, hoping that, perhaps he would be excited to see her, too.

*

Dai knocked on her door just before two-thirty; she'd been waiting for twenty minutes already. When she opened it, she was pleased to see he was wearing a proper t-shirt and trousers, not a vest and tracksuit bottoms. This was progress. He had his old trainers on, though.

"Hey, changed your mind about your new runners already, have you?"

"Don't want to mess them up," he said. "But you look nice."

"Yes, my footwear is particularly fetching today." She was wearing short, scarlet, wellington boots.

"Sensible," he said.

They walked down the stairs together, chatting, tapping on Paul's door on the way.

"He must already be down there," Dai said.

When they reached the ground floor, they found

Betty's door ajar, and let themselves through her flat to join the others outside. Betty's small flat smelt sweet and jammy, and there were cakes cooling on the side in the kitchen. They could hear voices from the garden. As they went out through her backdoor, Dai and April could see them stood near the shed: Jonty and Ben already pitching in to clear up, with Betty nearby, observing, clutching a bin bag. She had her back to them.

Everyone cheered when they saw April and Dai with their new haircuts, and Dai with his clean shave. Betty looked delighted and clasped her hands together. April and Dai bowed and curtseyed, and Ben wolf-whistled in response. Jonty even came over and gave Dai a hug. April looked around, surprised not to find Paul amongst them.

"My dear," Betty said. "It is always lovely to see you. Those are wonderful wellingtons."

"And lovely to see you, Betty. I shall miss our chats when I'm back at work."

"So shall I," she said.

"But where's Paul? I thought he was already here."

"He'll be here in a minute. He is bringing a friend, a young lady, I understand. I believe he has gone to collect her."

Chapter Thirty-Three: Paul

When Paul arrived at Betty's flat with Rosie, the others were already working hard to clear the remnants of the shed. He spotted Dai with his clean-shaven face and fashionable cropped hair. He was amazed, and pleased, to see him that way, and now understood, with relief, why April had been so secretive and excitable when he saw them together the day before. She had a hand in this.

"Who's this handsome fella you're hanging out with?" he called to her

But April did not appear to hear him, and carried on wrestling with a damaged box, trying to lift it, whole, over to the boot of Jonty's car, when it wasn't truly in one piece. The bottom was disintegrating, sides ripping, and singed note pads and pieces of paper were falling through the gaps. She had her back to him, but he could nonetheless tell she was exasperated. He was about to go and help her, but Rosie was already running over.

Rosie tapped her on the shoulder, and, with a jump, April dropped the box altogether. She looked at her in surprise and then over to Paul. She waved and beamed at him before hugging Rosie enthusiastically. She skipped over the rubble and fragments to where he stood.

"Nice of you to finally show up," she said.

"I was collecting our honoured guest," he replied.

"Ah yes, when Betty said you were… well, for a moment…"

He frowned. "For a moment…?"

"Oh, nothing. No matter. And what do you think of my handiwork with Dai?" She glanced over to where he stood, smiling proudly. "He scrubs up OK, doesn't he?"

Dai was bending over, pulling at something that seemed to be trapped. The sleeves of his t-shirt were rolled as high as they would go, exposing the curve of his biceps as they flexed and relaxed. His black tattoo peeped out, sharp and bold. One hair curl dropped across his brow.

"Yes. It's in the genes," Paul joked, one hand rubbing over his own head. "I always knew there was a handsome fellow hiding underneath there," he said, wondering why he had chosen this moment to start using the word 'fellow'. "Anyway, let me get myself sorted, and I'll join in."

He had a small rucksack in his hand, containing gloves and an old pair of boots. He waited for her to laugh or tease him, but she didn't. She stood before him and still had a vague smile on her face, her expression inscrutable.

*

They worked for well over ninety minutes, before Betty forced them to stop for cold glasses of water which they all received gratefully.

April and Rosie had raked and gathered fragments of paper and fabric into a heap, and then filled three bin bags full of it. Paul and Dai picked up the shattered pieces that were left of the shed itself, dislodging the parts of the sides and door that remained attached to the ground, either dug in or sunk into concrete. At one stage, Dai drop-kicked one stubborn piece violently, and Paul wondered if his mood had shifted again, but then Dai celebrated his success by doing a victory dance and holding his hands aloft as a champion. Paul high-fived him.

Betty called out to him, "My dear David, we'll have you skilled with a toolkit at this rate."

Dai laughed. "Unlikely... Hey, I think that's my punch bag!" he said, glancing over Paul's shoulder.

Rosie was trying to pick up a heavy black disc. It looked like a small, fat tyre. Each time she managed to grab one side of it she would lose her grip and drop it again. Dai walked over and kicked the debris around her, picking at fragments of red leather amongst the sand and ash. He picked up the black base confidently and walked it over to the boot of the Jeep. Rosie was agog.

"You need to teach me your ways," she said. "That thing weighed a ton. How on earth did you pick it up so gracefully?"

He was standing by the vehicle, leaning against it. "What, that little thing?"

Rosie and April laughed and nudged each other. Paul looked from them to Dai.

"Hey, Dai, I think you might want to see this." It was Ben.

Everyone stopped and went over to him. He was holding a photograph which, remarkably, seemed to be intact. He gripped the edges between finger and thumb of each hand, holding it up to examine the print. Dai came and stood next to him amongst the ash, and the pair of them stood with their heads dipped close together, fascinated by the little image. Ben let go of one corner and passed it to Dai.

"I don't believe it," Dai murmured. "I've not seen this in years."

Paul was eager to see the photo, too, but knew it was only right to let him have this moment, whatever it was. He stood nearby, waiting patiently for a sign to step forward.

"Mate, look at this," Dai said. He held the picture out to him.

It was a blurred colour print, the surface thick and grainy. Standing straight and serious was a young child of five or six, with slightly flared corduroy trousers, grubby cheeks, and curly black hair. There was a man, no more than forty, with a large dark moustache, spiky hair, longer at the back, and a cigarette hanging limply from his lips. Next to him was a woman of similar age with backcombed, heavily lacquered hair. She was beaming at the camera, head tilted and lovely. She had one arm around her husband and the other around an older woman with a puckered brow, dressed in a loose, paisley print dress.

He felt his hand start to shake, and Dai place his over it. They stood together, holding the picture firm.

"It's Aunty Doreen," Paul said. "She looks so happy, Dai." He looked at Dai to see him grinning, captivated by the image, and he felt the tears come over him as he allowed himself to mourn her for the first time.

*

They went back to work and it was another two hours before they were able to down tools. Everyone mercilessly teased Jonty who had said early on that it should take no more than fifty minutes now that Rosie had joined them. His Jeep, its back seats down, was loaded with bags of debris on top of an old sheet. They could fit no more in and had mounded five extra bags in a heap in the corner of the garden. The walls of the shed were gone, as were all the old boxes and suitcases and much of the ash. But the concrete base of the shed was still there, scorched and cracked, and there was no disguising the hint of an old fire around and about them.

Betty had been working away in the kitchen for the last half an hour. She had taken Ben away briefly to start the barbecue coals earlier, and had been discreetly loading the table with sauces, serviettes, and salads. The scent of firelighters and smoke was around them. When everyone stopped to admire their work, she ordered them all inside to wash up.

"It's the only way I can be sure that you will stop," she said. "And you really must stop now. You have worked hard enough. I am ever so grateful."

Dai touched her gently on the arm.

By the time they came back, a crocodile of obedient workers, she had placed a clutch of wine glasses on the table as well.

"Come on, I think it's time you had a reward for your labour. Would you open this for me, Paul?"

She passed him a bottle of sparkling wine. He resisted the urge to check the label and started to peel the foil away. There was a little splatter of applause when he popped the cork and steam rose from the bottle neck, and then he set about pouring the wine.

There was just enough for a small glass each. It felt like an enormous treat after their hard work.

"Cheers," Jonty said, raising his glass.

"To us," joined in Ben. Everyone took a healthy swig.

"Oh, and also to April. She should be celebrating, too," Dai added.

"Really? Why's that?" Paul asked. "It's not your birthday, is it?"

She shook her head, swallowing hard.

"Haven't you told them?" Dai looked at April, then back around at the group. "She's buying herself a flat."

The sharp, dry wine caught in Paul's throat. He gave a short cough. "I... I didn't realise you were looking to buy," he said. "Congratulations." He coughed again. "I was just getting used to having you around. Um... we'll miss you." He lifted his glass.

April smiled. "You're not getting rid of me that easily, I'm afraid. The flat isn't even built yet and, even then, I'm not going to live in it. At least, not immediately."

"Oh, really?" he asked. "You'll be renting it out, will you?"

"I've always wanted to be someone's landlord," she answered, nudging Dai.

Paul raised a quizzical eyebrow, still unsure what the story was.

"Yup," Dai said. "She's renting it to me."

Chapter Thirty-Four:
April

April enjoyed the little frisson that rippled through the group at her news; or perhaps it was Dai's news.

They had been to see the site plans and the show home yesterday, after their haircuts. Kelly was right: the flats were beautiful, in their way, and unusually spacious for modern new-builds. She had been impressed by the many features of efficiency and space-saving: they seemed excellent investments, each with a little outside area and a covered parking space. They were eco-friendly: well-insulated and with high quality materials: there were even charging points for eco-bikes. But she had known before she started that she was unlikely to want to move in there herself. It was not her style to buy a home that was ready fitted with laminate floor, spotlights, regularly shaped rooms. Her last flat, and Hummingbird House, had made that clear to her.

However, the flat sale had actually resulted in a good return and, during her chat with Dai, it had struck her she should do the supremely 'grown up thing' of investing in property. That actually, this was an option for her. And it would be all her own. When it transpired that Joy worked for the company in charge of the building project, it seemed all signs were pointing towards her buying one.

They had been lucky that Joy offered to meet them both and show them around. April gathered it wasn't common practice for her to give the site tours, but she teased Joy that if she did, they'd get even more sales: her fantastic enthusiasm and knowledge about all the materials used, and why each had been chosen, had convinced both Dai and April that the flat was a steal. No corners had been cut.

It was a complex stacked full of flats, a sort of puzzle of tessellating apartments neatly jigsawed together. There were six floors in each block, making thirty flats per building, each mirroring the other. It was overwhelming to contemplate, but there was a shop nearby, there would be a small playground for children, and there was a shared landscaped garden, too. There were saplings and raised flower beds. So, there was some semblance of home, and community.

"Perfect for you and your amazing horticulture skills," she teased him.

"So, what do you think?" Joy asked, as they returned to the entrance of the plot.

"I think this is a very sensible investment. What about you?" she asked Dai. "You're the one who is considering moving here. Can you imagine it? It's not exactly Hummingbird House. You probably wouldn't know your neighbours from Adam."

"I think this might be what I need, though. Low maintenance, clean, simple. And it's perfect for work. I can walk in."

"It's completely different, that's for sure," April said.

"Not a bad thing," he replied.

April had been surprised that Dai had so readily agreed to view the flat with her in the first place. After all, although they had spent the summer in the same property, they'd had only that one intimate conversation. But the fire had somehow shifted the dynamic, creating a familiarity between them — affection, even — that came from that shared experience. It seemed that he trusted her. And he was now ready to consider moving on.

Everything, almost everything, was falling into place.

Chapter Thirty-Five:
Betty

As Betty started to tidy up the dirty plates and sauce bottles from the garden table, she could hear Paul's friend, Rosie, telling the story of her marriage. Everyone listened with reverence, sat about the table. Betty went in and out unobtrusively, leaving a new bottle of wine on the table during one of her trips, placing it in front of Jonty who she knew would get straight to opening it.

Rosie's history was one of love at first sight, passion, and infertility. It was a raw, bleak story. Betty wondered at young people these days, marvelling at this. They were willing to share so much so quickly. There were pros and cons to it, she reasoned. Betty had to squish down and lock up her own story for years, and felt jealous of the ease with which this Rosie unpacked her tale in front of the residents of Hummingbird House, some of whom she had not long met.

But then, there were no secrets these days. Little privacy. Betty rather missed that.

"So, there you are," Rosie was saying, with a tear pooling on her upper lip. "That's the story of me and Mickey, and the babies we never had."

"Wow," April said, her eyes glassy too as she took a sip of wine. "That is extraordinary. I am so sorry."

She leaned into Paul, Betty noticed, and he stroked her arm affectionately.

"I guess we all have our stories, don't we?" David said, quietly.

"Yes, but I'm happy now," Rosie said, laughing through her tears. "Honest. Contrary to appearances." She wiped her face. "Only hummingbirds mate for life."

Betty walked into the kitchen with the last of the rubbish and condiments. It wasn't true what she had said, though. Hummingbirds do not mate for life. Luckily for them, and us, there are always second chances in love, and passion, and beauty. Everyone gets a myriad of opportunities if they keep their eyes wide and their mind open, and are willing to recognise and seize them.

She thought then of her Arthur, her poor dear Arthur, and the short, precious three years she had with him before he left.

She went back outside to get herself a drink. It was only going to be her second of the night, though no one seemed to have noticed. There were no chairs empty, just one small space on the bench. She poured herself a glass and stood, listening to the chatter of the group.

"Oh!" Paul said. "Sit down, Betty." He went to rise from his place on the bench.

"No, no," she said. "I shan't be staying long."

"Here," April said, getting up from her chair. She moved and sat precariously on the arm of the bench next to Paul. He put his hand out as if to steady her, Betty noted. As if to catch her. Or perhaps they would lean on each other.

"Thank you, dear." She sat.

199

"You sure you're comfortable, April?" Paul asked.

"So, what's your story, Paul?" It was Rosie.

"What do you mean, my story?"

"I think we know how April and Dai both ended up here. What about you?"

"Subtle as always, Rosie," April teased.

Paul blushed, taking a large swig from his glass. "I'm thoroughly boring," he said. "You don't want to hear from me."

"On the contrary, we do!" Jonty said. "Five years you've been here, and I still haven't learned your back story."

"And, believe me, he's speculated," Ben said.

"Merchant Navy, Foreign Legion, male model…" Jonty said, counting his ideas off on his fingers.

"I was young and foolish…" Paul muttered.

"'And I needed the money,'" Dai finished. Everyone laughed.

"Do you mind? There are ladies here," Paul said.

"Where?" Jonty asked. "Oh, Betty, you mean." April cried out in protest. "Oh, that reminds me. Is it time for strawberry shortcake, by any chance? Please, Betty? Pretty please?"

"You and your strawberry shortcake," Ben said, looking at him affectionately.

"I shall just finish my drink and then it's all yours," Betty said, glad to have made a contribution of sorts.

While Ben and Jonty were teasing each other over calories and who had eaten the most, Paul was speaking to April, murmuring out of earshot, gesturing. April leaned back over the arm of the chair, nodding, grinning, then got up and squeezed into the small gap on the bench beside him. He lifted his arm, this time properly placing it around her. She was crammed tight into the gap, her legs crossed and her hand gently resting on his thigh. She snuggled in, looked up at his face, so close to hers, with a smile, and then rested her head on his shoulder.

Betty finished her small glass of wine and carefully got up again, aware that the light was now dim and the garden still battered by the water and debris of the fire.

She walked back to the kitchen to collect the cake, taking her glass with her, wondering if they would be holding hands, or even kissing, by the time she made it back out again. Thinking of first impressions and second chances.

Sometimes, she thought, it was truly wonderful to be the landlady of Hummingbird House.

Enjoyed this? Please leave a review:

Goodreads

Amazon - U.K.

Amazon - .Com

About the Author

Jane Harvey is a pen name. 'Jane' crafts fun fiction for the thinking woman, where she enjoys exploring unexpected friendships and writing happy endings. This is lucky, because in real life her (prize-winning) fiction is a little bleaker. She was born and raised on the island of Jersey.

https://instagram.com/jane_harvey_novelist
https://facebook.com/janeharveynovelist

Acknowledgements

Thank you to my beta readers: Anne, Karen, and my mum, Mary. Thank you to my ARC crew social media writer friends – many of whom I have never met but will always support. And so much gratitude to you, my lovely reader.

Jane Harvey is the pen name of Dreena Collins

Dreena Collins writes literary short stories

ALSO BY
Dreena Collins

Available at: <u>Read – dreenawriting</u> or via Amazon.

- o **She Had Met Liars Before**: Six Very Short Stories of Strength and Survival

- o **Taste: Six of the Best** (Six Readers' Favourites from previous works)

- o **Collected** (The Complete Stories: The Blue Hour Series plus Bird Wing)

- o **The Day I Nearly Drowned** (Short Stories Vol. Two)

- o **The Blue Hour** (Short Stories Vol. One)

Introducing Dreena's micro-collection, **She Had Met Liars Before**. Six Very Short Stories of Strength and Survival.

Turn over for a short taste of the opening story…

The (Almost Entirely True) Story of Jessie and the Mountain

Jessie would not go.

They told her that she had to move. The mountain, *y mynydd*, was sliding ever closer: inching and scuttling shingle and stone, until one day it would subside. It was for her own good, they said. Her safety.

She stood in her porch, looked up towards the peak, mottled in purples, greys, greens. They talked as if it was sly, this crag. Not to be trusted. And it was steep and splintered, sharp – but it was a confident landscape. Reassuring.

These men did not worry her. She had met liars before.

She was *dewr*, she was cynical. 18 cats at her feet.

A hundred residents had already left, or more. The men were quick to knock down what they could. Of the few houses left, most were abandoned and hollow; the remains of the terrace had slipped into disarray. Doors and windows boarded or broken - casements gaping into black rooms like a row of rotten teeth...

Buy **She Had Met Liars Before** here: Read – dreenawriting

Made in the USA
Middletown, DE
06 July 2022